Gorgon & Gambit

Gorgon & Gambit

Book 2
A Serpent & Spice Adventure

SYLVIE D. HARLOWE

For Emma.
You inspire me every day.
Keep dreaming.

CONTENTS

1	A Thread of Blue	1
2	The Silent Fortress	8
3	A Lie in the Sunlight	12
4	The Dark Descent	20
5	A Pocket of Darkness	28
6	A Sacred Reflection	34
7	The Weighted Chart	40
8	Skeletal Hill	43
9	A Rain of Stone	48
10	The Death of a Name	54
11	The Turn of the Tide	59
12	Leverage and Lies	62
13	A Shared Rhythm	66
14	Lesson in Logistics	74
15	The Price of Privacy	79
16	A Vessel of Oil	84
17	The Frayed Hem	91
18	The Marble Facade	98
19	The Silken Net	104
20	A Reflection of Victory	116
21	The Truth in Stone	126
22	The Sealed Message	129

CHAPTER 1
A Thread of Blue

Three Months Later.

The sun cleared the cliffs of Issa, pressing a heavy, warm blanket on her eyelids, a promise that the day would be hot. Salt and the sharp scent of hillside lavender drifted through the open shutters. The only sounds were the hum of bees in the garden and the barest rustle of linen.

Lyrra lay still, letting the morning settle in her. She kept her eyes closed, just breathing. In. Out. Unburdened. Ninety-four days had passed like this, each one a quiet miracle that had slowly leached the stiffness from her spine. Beside her, Hanno slept, his breathing a deep, even rhythm of safety. The heat of him was an anchor, solid and real as the land itself. She tucked her hand into the crease of his hip, and drifted back into a deeper, more peaceful sleep.

When she woke again, the light was brighter, throwing a heavy, butter-yellow light across the whitewashed walls of their bedroom. Her hand slid across the sheets, searching for his warmth. She found only cool, empty linen.

A scar of old fear ached in her chest. Coldness. Then she heard it—the rhythmic scrape-and-pull of a knife against twine from outside on the veranda. A now-familiar and comforting sound that dissolved her tension, allowing a long, slow exhale.

She slipped from the bed, wrapping herself in a fresh linen tunic. Hanno was already outside, seated on a low stool, his back to her. His hands, which she knew could be so strong, moved with a quiet, practiced efficiency, mending a tear in a fishing net.

The stone of the veranda was warm beneath her bare feet. She leaned against the doorframe, just watching him for a moment. The sun was already climbing over the deep, defiant blue of the sea, catching the dark curls of his hair.

He must have felt her watching him. He paused his work and looked over his shoulder, a slow, easy smile transformed his face. "You're awake."

"I was wondering where you went," she said, walking toward him.

He set the net aside and reached for a small clay bowl on the table beside him, while pulling her into the space between his knees. He held out a single, perfect fig, its purple skin taut and glistening with the promise of sweet nectar. "I saved you the best one."

She took it, her fingers grazing the calloused skin of his palm. He didn't let go. He pulled her closer, his other hand finding her waist, and tilted his head up. He moved his mouth closer, his breath lingering with notes of sweetness. The kiss tasted of him— salt and sweet, sticky fig.

o   o   o   o   o

Later, they walked down to the port market. The air under the bright sun was a mess of smells and sounds—the clean brine of the sea, the sharp scent of gutted fish, the shouting of merchants, and the piercing cries of gulls.

Hanno's hand rested on the small of her back as they moved through the throng. It wasn't a gesture of ownership, the way Gisco's had been, but of simple, unwavering presence. A fixed point of warmth in the chaos of the crowd.

Ahead, a cheer went up from a small crowd gathered around a fish stall. Niko, a young fisherman with shoulders like oak and a voice that could carry across the water, was grinning, holding up a massive, silver-scaled tuna for all to see.

Lyrra leaned into Hanno, a small, sharp smile touching her lips as she murmured, "He reminds me of that merchant in Carthage who claimed his silks were woven by nymphs."

His words vibrated against her back, his breath warm against her skin. "At least Niko's fish is real. I'm still not convinced about those silks."

A quiet warmth bloomed in her chest. The simple joy of it—a secret shared in plain sight. As they paused to watch Niko's performance, Hanno's thumb began to idly rub a small circle on her back, a thoughtless, comforting motion. But then the motion stilled for a single, sharp beat. Lyrra glanced up at him. His focus shifted over her shoulder, distant and hard, his gaze fixing on something in the bustling harbor. The warmth from his hand on her back seemed to recede, leaving a patch of sudden coolness on her skin. She looked up at the sky, seeking a reason for it, but the sun was bright, sailing high above a few thin wisps of cloud. It offered no answers. Just as quickly, the warmth returned to his eyes. He looked down at her, his hand tightening on her back in a gesture that felt both protective and possessive. They were a silent fortress for two in the middle of the bustling crowd. *Just us.*

The dim, cool air of Theodora's tavern was a welcome relief from the afternoon heat. It smelled of woodsmoke, old wine, and the rich, savory stew that was the innkeeper's specialty. Theodora, a woman whose sharp eyes missed nothing, was wiping down the heavy wooden counter, her movements efficient and devoid of fuss.

As Hanno ordered their dinner, a local woman Lyrra knew only as Adrasteia slid up beside them. She appraised Lyrra from head to toe, a slow, deliberate look that felt like a physical touch.

"Three months he's had you here, girl," Adrasteia said, her voice coated with a false sweetness. "Has he not made an honest woman of you yet?"

A familiar coldness, a phantom echo of her mother's judgment, pricked at Lyrra's skin. Her shoulders tensed. Before she could form a reply, Theodora slammed a heavy bronze ladle down on the counter. The sound was a sharp crack in the tavern's low hum.

Her voice, when it came, was as sharp as a shard of pottery. "His honesty is between him and the gods, Adrasteia. Tanit knows her honor is her own. Your business is with the bottom of that empty cup. Now, move along."

Adrasteia sputtered for a moment, then scurried away into the tavern's gloom.

A sudden heat flooded Lyrra's chest, fierce and unfamiliar. She looked at Theodora's stern profile, at the worn wood of the counter, at Hanno's steady presence beside her. *This*, she thought. *This is real.*

Hanno broke the silence, his tone light as he turned back to Theodora. "You're saving us seats for dinner, I hope? We came for your famous stew."

Lyrra played along, the tension in her shoulders finally melting away. "The one that could be used to patch a hole in a ship's hull?"

A grin spread across Hanno's face. "That's the one." But as he spoke, his eyes shifted toward the tavern's shadowed corner, and the warmth in them was simply … gone. Lyrra caught the shift, a momentary dissonance she couldn't place, before he met her eyes again, his smile firmly back in place. "Try to look like you enjoy it this time. You're terrible at hiding your face."

His teasing pulled her back into the safety of their private world. The coil of tension in her shoulders finally eased.

o   o   o   o   o

As evening fell, the light in the villa turned soft and orange, the air cooling with the promise of night. A trader from a Carthaginian vessel had come and gone, leaving behind a bolt of silk. Hanno unfurled it across their table. Deep blue. The color of a twilight sea. It was heavy and cool to the touch, a luxury Lyrra had almost forgotten.

She ran her hand over it, the slide of the fabric a ghost of a life she no longer missed. But the craftsmanship was undeniable. Her fingers traced the selvedge, appreciating the fine, even work, and

5

then snagged on a tiny, raised knot of thread. A flaw in such a perfect piece?

She leaned in, her eyes narrowing. It wasn't a flaw. It was a shape. Her breath stopped. *No. By Tanit's loom, it couldn't be.*

Her hand flattened on the silk, as if to smother the image before it could be real. Woven into the border, so small and fine it was almost invisible, was a story in thread. She reached out, her fingers trembling slightly as they traced the first tiny, intricate pictograph. Hanno saw the sudden, sharp shift in her posture and came to stand behind her, his hands resting on her shoulders, a firm, supportive weight.

Her voice was a quiet murmur, barely a whisper at first. "She got our message," she breathed, her finger tracing the simple outline of the Greek peninsula and, to the west of it, the unmistakable outline of a ship. "She knows we're here. She knows we're safe."

Her finger moved to the next image: a woman's face, a thorny vine twisting out from between her lips. "Sybil," tumbled out of her mouth. The name was a drop of poison in the warm room. "She's still there. Still twisting the truth."

The third image was a small, intricately woven spiderweb. At its very center, where the spider would be, was a single key. Lyrra stared at it for a long moment, the meaning clicking into place, her voice now filled with a new, profound respect. "She's weaving them together: The cooks in the kitchens, the workers in the market, the men on the docks. They're the threads of her web. And the key—" she looked up, her wide eyes finding his in the reflection of the darkening window. "The key means she is at the center. She holds their trust—and uses what they see and hear to unlock secrets. Leverage."

Her finger stopped on the final image: a tiny loom with a single, unbroken thread of deep blue—the exact color of the silk they held—stretching away from it. A small, watery smile touched her lips. "She remembers the pattern I taught her," she whispered, her finger gently touching the blue thread. "She's telling me the thread between us is unbroken."

A hot pressure built behind her eyes—for Asha's courage, for the friend she missed, for the thread that held them together across the sea. She pressed her hand flat over the embroidered story. Hanno's hand came down to cover hers, his warmth sudden and solid against her skin.

CHAPTER 2
The Silent Fortress

Hanno's hand held hers in the quiet of the villa. The embroidered story on the silk was a testament to a world of shadows and schemes, a world that felt a lifetime away. He didn't speak. He didn't need to. He simply turned her hand over in his and brought her palm to his lips, pressing a soft, firm kiss into its center.

It was enough. She turned from the table, stepping into his arms, her face fitting into the familiar place against his collarbone. He held her, his chin resting on the top of her head, his grip tight, a silent reinforcement.

For a long moment, they just stood there, breathing together in the fading light. He kissed the lingering chill of Carthage from her lips, replacing the phantom taste of fear and doubt with the warm reality of him.

He lifted her, his movements easy and sure, and carried her into the bedroom. Moonlight was beginning to spill through the open shutters, painting silver stripes across the cool floor and the simple linen sheets of their bed. He laid her down gently, and for a moment, just looked at her, his eyes dark with an emotion so deep it made her breath catch.

She saw the frantic hunger of their first nights was gone. Different. Deeper. She saw the lines around his eyes soften, the way his focus narrowed, as if the rest of the world had ceased to exist. This was the almost painful concentration of a man memorizing the one thing he could not bear to lose. *Her.*

His fingers, trembling almost imperceptibly, went to the ties of her tunic. His movements were slow, deliberate, an act of unwrapping something sacred. She mirrored him, her hands finding the worn linen of his own tunic, her knuckles brushing against the hard warmth of his chest. When they were finally bare in the moonlight, she reached for him, her fingers tracing the trails of old scars on his ribs, each one a path to a story she still didn't know.

He knelt on the bed, his mouth replacing her hand. His tongue traced a hot, wet path down the center of her body, and she shivered, not from cold, but from the sheer, focused intent in his touch. He settled between her legs, his breath a hot promise against her skin before he put his mouth on her. The rough scrape of his stubble on her inner thighs, the soft, wet slide of his tongue—the contrast made her hips tilt up instinctively. He knew her. He knew the maddening rhythm of long, slow strokes followed by a quick, circling flick that made a gasp tear from her throat. The only sounds were her ragged breaths and the low, focused hum from his throat—not of pleasure, but of a consuming concentration. Grounding. An act of a man trying to taste his own salvation.

The feeling was a gathering in her belly, a white-hot point of tension tightening and tightening until her vision blurred at the edges. The world narrowed to the pressure of his mouth, the linen scraping her back, the muscles in her thighs quivering beyond her control. She cried out his name as the tension shattered, splintering through her, a violent release that split her from the inside. The aftershocks left her skin so sensitive that the cool night air felt like a thousand tiny needles of pleasure.

He moved up her body, his mouth finding hers, and she tasted herself on his lips—a shocking, intimate taste that was not just accepted, but savored. It sent a fresh tremor through her. He started to move, to settle between her legs, but she met his kiss with a smile. She placed a hand flat on his chest.

And pushed.

The surprise in his eyes was followed by a look of complete, willing surrender. He lay back without resistance, his hands falling to his sides, giving her everything. She straddled his hips, her hair falling around them like a dark curtain, and took him in her mouth.

This was her turn. Her game. She delighted in the raw, uncontrolled groan that tore from his throat, in the way his hips bucked into her touch. She teased him, learning the exact angle and pressure of her tongue that made his control snap. *There*, she thought with a thrill of pure, joyful power. *That spot, right there, is his undoing.* This wasn't just giving pleasure; it was Lyrra wielding her expertise, celebrating the beautiful, vulnerable truth of this strong man.

When she moved to straddle his waist, she lowered herself onto him, a slow, deliberate slide that made him hiss through his teeth. The stretching pressure of him filled her completely. She leaned forward, her forehead resting against his, their eyes locked in the dim light. And she saw it. She saw the adoration, yes, but beneath it was a fierce, desperate vow. The ghost was there, in the back of his eyes—the man who knew how quickly a sanctuary could burn.

She began to move, a slow, deep, controlling rhythm, watching his face, watching his soul laid bare for her. But it was too much for him. The desperation won. In one powerful, fluid motion, his hands clamped on her waist and he rolled them, pinning her beneath him without breaking their connection.

The rhythm shattered. This was no longer a slow dance; it was a primal, driving need. He thrust into her, hard and deep, not with anger, but with a frantic urgency, as if he could physically drive the rest of the world away. She met every slam of his hips with a fierce, joyful abandon, her nails digging into the hard muscle of his shoulders. Their breathing grew harsh, their names breaking from their lips, an anchor in the storm of sensation.

She felt his orgasm begin a second before her own, a deep, internal clench. His name was a choked, guttural cry against her neck as he poured himself into her, and she captured her own cry with his mouth, a simultaneous, shuddering release.

He collapsed on top of her, a dead weight of pure satisfaction, and did not withdraw. He buried his face in the curve of her neck, his breathing loud and ragged in her ear. She could feel him still inside her, softening, the scent of them—musky, salty, and warm—a comforting blanket. This was their sanctuary. Not a place, but this. This shared, slick stillness.

"Lyrra," his voice broke. The single word was a prayer, a promise, and a plea all at once. She just held him, her heart hammering against his, safe in the quiet heart of a sleeping island.

CHAPTER 3
A Lie in the Sunlight

The next day broke with the same lazy warmth, the scent of the sea mingling with the smell of toasted bread and honey from their small kitchen. They ate on the veranda, their knees occasionally brushing each other's under the simple wooden table, their conversation flowing with an easy, purposeless rhythm. They spoke of nothing and everything: the price of olives, a leaking roof tile, the absurd pride of a fisherman named Niko. The peace between them was a simple, uncalculated ease.

Later, they made their way down to the port. The late morning sun had burned the last of the dew from the stones on the path. The walk was steep and winding, and the smell of pine and hot dust slowly gave way to the sharp, briny tang of the harbor. The quiet hum of the hills was replaced by the growing cacophony of a working port—the shouts of sailors, the creak of rigging, the rumble of carts over stone. Hanno took her hand as they entered the press of the crowd, a comfortable, practiced gesture that felt like an extension of her own body.

The full, vibrant chaos of the market slammed into them. They found Niko near the docks, already holding court, his voice booming over the noise as he recounted his latest triumph at sea. Hanno caught Lyrra's eye, a shared look of amusement passing between them, and they joined the small crowd, content to listen.

They were still laughing at Niko's exaggerated tale of wrestling the great tuna into his boat, the sound easy and bright in the afternoon sun. Lyrra felt Hanno's chest rumble with another laugh behind her, his hand warm on her back.

She was still smiling when she realized he wasn't.

His laughter stopped. It was cut off mid-breath. The warmth in his eyes, which had been crinkled with amusement, vanished, leaving something cold and hard she had never seen before. His whole posture shifted, his shoulders squaring not with confidence, but with a rigid, defensive tension.

"Hanno?" she whispered, her smile faltering.

He didn't answer. His attention was fixed on the harbor below, where a new ship had just rounded the point. It was a sleek, fast trireme, its single, dark sail bearing no sigil of trade. It moved with the lean, predatory grace of a warship.

Lyrra looked in the same direction as a man began to disembark, moving with the straight-line purpose of a soldier, a stark contrast to the ambling merchants and sailors. He wore no polished Roman armor, but a dark, burnished breastplate, Greek in style, practical and deadly. As he stepped into a patch of direct sun, something glinted on its center.

A sigil. The head of a Gorgon, its bronze snakes seeming to writhe in the light.

The warmth of the fish and wine in her stomach instantly vanished, replaced by a cold, heavy dread. She didn't know the symbol, but she knew what it meant. It was a promise of violence.

She looked back at Hanno. His face had tightened, the easy lines around his eyes hardening into a grim network of focus. The old scar on his brow stood out, a pale, jagged line against his suddenly taut skin.

"What is it?" she asked again, her voice barely audible. "Who is that?"

He didn't look at her. His eyes were fixed on the man on the dock. "They call him the Gorgon." The name, a near exhale.

He blinked, and the stranger in his eyes was gone. He looked down at her as his mouth formed the shape of a smile, but the muscles around his eyes remained hard and flat.

"It's nothing, Lyrra." His voice was low and flat, stripped of all warmth. "We're leaving. Now."

He didn't wait for an answer. His hand, which had been resting on her back, now gripped her waist. The touch was firm, insistent, not a request. He turned her away from the harbor, away from the man with the Gorgon on his chest. He clapped Niko on the shoulder with a clipped, "We'll see you for dinner," and began walking them away from the market, his pace just a little too fast.

Lyrra went with him, her heart hammering against her ribs.

He was lying.

The man on the dock was anything but *nothing*. The sudden, cold wall between her and Hanno felt more dangerous than any stranger in the port.

His pace was too fast, his fingers digging into the soft flesh of her waist, pulling her through the market in a blur of shouting vendors and flapping awnings. She had to half-jog to keep up, her sandals slapping against the worn cobblestones. The lie was a stone in her throat. The feeling of being managed—a cage snapping shut around her. And the fire, the one she thought had been banked to a gentle warmth, roared back to life.

She stopped.

The abrupt halt pulled him up short. He turned, his face a mask of controlled urgency, a flash of raw frustration in his eyes.

"Lyrra, not here," he said, his voice a low, urgent hiss meant only for her. "We have to go."

She met his eyes, her own voice quiet but unyielding, a core of steel he had helped her forge. "No. In Carthage, you promised me we would go at my speed. You promised me the truth. That man on the dock is not *nothing*. You are lying to me, and I refuse to be protected like a child. Wherever you are going, I am going with you."

It was a silent stalemate, waged in the heart of the bustling market. She saw the conflict in his eyes—the desperate need to shield her warring with the undeniable truth of her words. She locked her eyes on his, letting him see her unbreakable resolve, the same resolve that had brought down a house in Carthage.

The fight went out of him. His shoulders slumped in a barely perceptible motion, and he gave a single, sharp, defeated nod.

He was no longer protecting her; he was walking side by side with his partner into danger.

He turned, and this time she walked with him. His hand fell from her waist, and the space between them was charged with a new, sober tension. His pace was still fast, but it was different now—a predator's economy of motion, not a panicked flight.

The vibrant sounds of the market faded as he led them away from the port and into the narrow, winding backstreets of the town. The world shifted. Lyrra felt her own senses sharpen, her focus narrowing to match his. She was seeing the world through his eyes now. Every shadowed doorway was a potential ambush. Every overhanging balcony was a perch. The air, which had tasted of salt and freedom only moments before, now felt heavy with threat.

She watched the shift in him, the way his shoulders settled, the way his restless eyes were constantly sweeping the rooftops and alley mouths. The easygoing merchant was gone, stripped away to reveal something harder, older, and infinitely more dangerous underneath. The man walking beside her was no longer her lover. He was a predator, and this world of shadows was his hunt.

She should have been terrified. A part of her was. But a deeper, stronger part felt a grim satisfaction. This was real. This was the truth of the man she loved, the sharp, dangerous edges he had tried to keep hidden from her. And she was not being shielded from it.

He led her to an alley behind Theodora's tavern, the air thick with the smell of refuse and damp stone. She followed him in without hesitation.

A man was leaning against the far wall, casually sharpening a long, wicked-looking knife with a whetstone. The soft, rhythmic *shing-shing-shing* of steel on stone was the only sound. He looked up as they entered, and his eyes, the color of chips of slate, flicked from Hanno to her. It was a slow, appraising glance that took in everything.

"Well, well," the man said, his voice a dry rasp. "Hanno."

"Lykaon," Hanno acknowledged plainly.

He didn't look at Hanno, his stare still fixed on Lyrra. "I see you've finally found a bed-warmer with better taste in clothes. And more spirit. This one looks like she'd actually bite."

Hanno didn't speak. He exploded.

He crossed the alley in two silent, predatory strides. There was a sharp clang of metal on stone as the knife was knocked from the man's hand, skittering into the shadows. Before Lyrra could even draw a breath, Hanno had slammed him back against the rough stone wall. Dust and grit rained down from the impact.

Lyrra didn't flinch. She didn't even breathe. She stood rooted to the stone, her eyes locked on the scene. The speed of it was what shocked her. The sound—a wet, solid thud of Hanno's forearm against the man's throat—sucked the air from the alley. This was not the man who saved her figs. She saw the chilling void in Hanno's eyes. The cold focus of a killer. *This is him*, a voice in her head whispered with a grim, final clarity. *This is the rest of him.* Her breath returned in a slow, steady exhale. Her hands, which had clenched into fists, relaxed at her sides. This was the truth she had demanded. Awe, cold and sharp, cut through her fear.

The two men were chest to chest, breathing hard, locked in a brutal transaction of muscle and memory. The man—Lykaon—didn't struggle. He just stared into Hanno's eyes with a look of weary, bitter recognition. His gaze was flat, unblinking—the stony stare that must have earned him his name.

"You will not talk about her," Hanno growled, his voice a low, dangerous sound she had never heard. "Ever. Now, tell me why you're here before I finish what we started in Thera."

Lykaon gave a wry, pained smile, his voice a strained rasp against Hanno's arm. "I was in Carthage. Missed you by a week. You left a mess." He coughed. "Been chasing whispers ever since. The trail went cold, until someone in the underground got word you were playing house on this forgotten rock. So I came."

Hanno's grip didn't lessen. "Why?"

"Telemon," Lykaon choked out.

The name was a seed of fear and violence planted in the quiet alley.

"He wants his rock back," Lykaon continued, his eyes never leaving Hanno's. "The Star of Emesa. And he wants you." He paused, a shift of something that might have been grim amusement in his eyes. "The problem is, the whole damn underground heard the whisper. He didn't just hire me."

Lyrra watched Hanno's face pale, the dread in his eyes palpable. "Melqart save us." Hanno's voice was tight. "Who did he send? The Scorpions of Crete? The Bronze Shields?"

Lykaon scoffed, a sound of pure professional disdain. "Please. He sent the ones who get paid by the pound and usually end up killing each other over the scraps. They're like vultures. No discipline." He glared at Hanno. "But even a vulture can get lucky. And there are a lot of them."

Hanno finally eased the pressure, taking a single, deliberate step back. The raw violence didn't vanish; it was just … sheathed. Lyrra watched the muscles in his shoulders remain coiled, his hands still fisted at his sides. He glanced at her, just for a second, and in his eyes she saw not an apology, but a grim question: *Are you still with me?*

Lykaon worked his jaw, rubbing the raw, red mark Hanno's arm had left on his throat. He didn't look injured; he looked annoyed, like a craftsman whose tool had been misused. His eyes scanned the grimy floor until he spotted his knife. He bent, retrieved it with a smooth, economical motion, and wiped the blade on his thigh before tucking it back into its sheath. The act was a quiet, definitive statement: the brawl was over; business had resumed.

His stare, now cold and serious, found Hanno again, measuring him. The buzzing tension in the alley shifted. It was no longer the threat of a fight between two men, but the shared, chilling weight of a hunt that had already begun. Lyrra could feel it in the sudden stillness, in the way both men now seemed to be listening for sounds beyond the alley walls.

"They're already here," Lykaon said, his voice now a flat, professional monotone. "Your ship is being watched. It's a trap."

He took a step out of the shadows, his eyes finding Lyrra's for a final, unreadable moment.

"Your little *holiday*, Hanno? This *quaint little life* you've built—" His gaze shifted back to the man he once called a friend. "It's over."

CHAPTER 4
The Dark Descent

The finality of Lykaon's words hung in the alley, a promise of violence that was already in motion. Hanno didn't hesitate. He grabbed Lyrra's arm, not with the bruising force of a man trying to manage her, but with a desperate, urgent grip.

"Theodora's," he said to Lykaon. It was a command, not a request.

They moved through the backstreets, a tense, silent unit. Hanno was a grim-faced phantom in the lead, Lykaon a watchful shadow at their back, and Lyrra in the middle, her mind struggling to reconcile the man who saved her a fig that morning with the predator now leading them into the shadows. The world had tilted on its axis. The man she loved was a creature of shadows and violence, and he was taking her deeper into his world with every step.

Hanno didn't go through the tavern's main entrance. He slipped through a side door that led directly into the heat and clatter of Theodora's kitchen. The innkeeper looked up from a steaming pot, her eyes narrowing at the sight of them—Hanno's grim face, the dangerous stranger behind him.

Hanno didn't explain. He pulled a heavy pouch of coins from his belt and dropped it on a flour-dusted worktable. The thud was loud in the small space.

"A private room," he said, his voice low and tight. "Now. No questions."

Theodora's gaze flicked from the desperation in Hanno's eyes to the silent, deadly presence of Lykaon, then to Lyrra. She saw the truth of the situation in a single, sharp glance. She gave a curt nod and pointed with her ladle toward a heavy wooden door at the back of the kitchen.

The room was a small, windowless wine storeroom, its air thick with the smell of old wood, dust, and the faint, sweet scent of spilled wine. The door closed behind them, the heavy bolt sliding home with a definitive thud.

Hanno began to pace the cramped space, a frantic, wasted energy in every step, his hands running through his hair. Lykaon, ever the professional, moved to the door, testing the lock, his eyes scanning the stone walls for any other point of weakness.

Lyrra stood perfectly still, her mind a quiet counterpoint to their chaotic energy, watching them both.

"We have to run," Hanno said, his voice a raw nerve. "Now. We get to the ship, we cut the lines, and we fight our way out of the harbor."

Lyrra heard the panic in his voice and saw the plan for what it was: not a strategy, but a prayer. A reckless charge born of his terror for her safety. He wasn't thinking like a tactician; he was thinking like a lover, and it would get them both killed.

Lykaon scoffed without turning from the door. "Fight our way out? With what? Those opportunistic jackals will be watching the harbor from the cliffs. They'll rain arrows on your deck before you can raise a sail. It's a suicide run."

Lyrra's voice cut through it, calm and focused.

"We can't leave without it, can we?" she said.

Both men stopped and looked at her.

"The Star of Emesa," she finished.

Hanno's jaw tightened. "It's in a hidden compartment in the captain's cabin. I can get to it in minutes, but I need time."

"Then you need a diversion," Lykaon said, turning from the door, a spark of professional interest in his eyes. "Something loud, bloody, and stupid enough to draw every hired knife in the port." He gave a humorless smirk. "A good old-fashioned tavern brawl over a gambling debt. They won't be able to resist."

"When?" Lyrra asked, her mind already working, seeing the shape of the plan. "If you start the brawl before we move, they'll be on high alert. You have to do it *while* we're on the ship. It has to pull them away from the harbor."

Lykaon's eyes narrowed, a new, grudging respect dawning on his face. He looked at Hanno, then back at Lyrra.

"She's right," he said, the words a simple statement of fact. "It's a better plan."

Hanno looked at Lyrra, truly looked at her, and she saw the predator in his eyes soften, replaced by a flicker of the awe she had seen in the alley. He gave a single, sharp nod. The plan was set.

o   o   o   o   o

Night fell, swallowing the vibrant colors of Issa in shades of charcoal and silver. From the grimy window of their storeroom, they watched the harbor. The moon was a sliver, a conspirator in their endeavor. Lykaon gave them a final, curt nod. "Give me until the third watch. Then make your move. And try not to get killed. It complicates my fee." He slipped out into the darkness.

They waited, the silence stretching thin. Then, the night erupted. A roar of fury from a tavern near the docks, followed by the splintering crash of wood and the unmistakable clang of drawn steel. The diversion had begun.

"Now," Hanno said, his voice a low command.

They moved through the shadows, a silent, disciplined unit, their feet silent on the stones. The harbor was a chaotic mess of running men and shouting voices, all drawn toward the brawl. *The Desert Wind* sat dark and silent at its mooring, a ghost ship in the moonlight.

They slipped aboard, their movements a synchronized dance of absolute trust. Hanno pointed to a shadowed alcove near the stern. Lyrra gave a single, sharp nod. He moved toward the captain's cabin. She counted three slow breaths before knocking a loose coil of rope to the deck on the opposite side of the ship. The sharp thud drew the attention of the single, bored-looking guard left on the dock, his head turning away from the cabin door for just a precious few seconds.

It was all Hanno needed. He was inside. Lyrra held her breath, her hand resting on the cool, familiar hilt of the dagger hidden in her tunic. Every second was a counted heartbeat in the silence.

He emerged from the cabin, a small, heavy-looking leather pouch now tucked into his belt. He gave her a quick, sharp nod. *Success.*

They were turning to leave when a shape detached itself from the shadows of the mainmast. It was a man, broad as an ox, a short, ugly-looking sword in his hand. One of the hunting dogs chasing them.

Hanno reacted instantly, shoving Lyrra behind him, his body a solid, living shield. The hunter lunged, his sword a blur of silver. Hanno met the attack with a brutal, close-quarters efficiency, deflecting the man's arm. A sharp crack echoed in the night as he broke the man's wrist. The hunter roared in pain, but he was strong, his other hand grabbing a fistful of Hanno's tunic, pulling him off balance.

He was raising a dagger for a killing blow when Lyrra moved. She didn't scream. She didn't hesitate. She drove her own dagger into the thick muscle of the man's thigh.

The blade met the thick resistance of his muscle, then slid deeper, finding its home in living flesh. A shocking wetness coated her hand—*his blood*—followed by a rush of warmth that spread up her arm. There was no horror. No regret. Only a cold and clear certainty. Her thought was sharp and absolute as the steel in her hand: *You will not take him from me.*

He bellowed, his grip on Hanno faltering. It was the opening Hanno needed. He drove his shoulder into the man's chest, sending him stumbling back toward the ship's railing. With a final shove, Hanno sent him over the side, a heavy splash echoing in the sudden silence.

But the fight had been too loud. Shouts were already rising from the dock. They were out of time.

Hanno's head snapped toward the sounds on the dock, his eyes wide, scanning. Deck. Railing. Water. Lyrra. His focus dropped to her hand, to her dagger, slick with blood. His eyes found hers again. His hand shot out and grabbed her, pulling her to the far side of the ship, away from the docks. His eyes locked on hers, his voice a ragged, urgent command. "Trust me."

She just held on tight as he pulled her with him, over the railing and into the shocking, cold blackness of the sea. The impact was a brutal, deafening roar. Cold water slammed into her, stealing the air from her lungs in a single, violent gasp. The light linen of her tunic instantly became a sodden shroud, clinging to her limbs, tangling her, dragging her down into the crushing weight of the sea.

Panic flared—a terrifying second of sinking into the absolute dark. Then Hanno's grip tightened on her hand and he was pulling, kicking, fighting for them both, dragging her upward toward the distant, silvery surface of the moon. They broke the surface together, a shared, desperate gasp for air. Her lungs burned. The shouts from the dock were a distant, muffled noise, swallowed by the vast, dark silence of the harbor.

"Swim," he gasped, his voice a raw sound in the night. The swim was a black and timeless agony. The sea was in her nose, her throat, at once slick and sharp, a coating of brine that burned her tongue raw. The only real thing in the universe was Hanno's hand, his grip. An unbreakable promise. He was the power pulling her through the water, his strokes cutting through the chop toward the waiting shape of Lykaon's ship.

It felt like an eternity. Her arms ached, her legs were leaden, but she held onto him, matching his rhythm as best she could. Finally, rough, splintery wood was beneath her grasping fingers. A pair of strong hands seized her under the arms, hauling her unceremoniously from the sea.

She collapsed onto the deck, a heap of soaking linen and trembling limbs, coughing up a lungful of stinging saltwater. Hanno landed beside her, just as spent, his chest heaving. They were alive. They had the stone.

A pair of simple leather sandals appeared in her line of sight. A woman knelt beside her, silent and efficient. Lyrra looked up, her mind automatically sorting the woman into a familiar box: quiet, still, gaze lowered. *A slave*, the thought was instant, a product of her upbringing. *Someone of no account.*

The woman wrapped the blanket around her, her touch surprisingly firm, her movements competent. Then her hand rested on Lyrra's shoulder, a steadying weight. She looked up, and her eyes met Lyrra's.

Lyrra had expected a servant's gaze—blank, or perhaps curious. She did not expect this. She did not expect to be so completely *seen*. The woman's eyes held no judgment, only a quiet, knowing stillness. A recognition.

"The sea gives back what it does not want," the woman said, her voice a low, calm alto, as if commenting on the tide. "It seems it does not want you, tonight. At least not yet."

The words were so strange, so unexpected, that they short-circuited Lyrra's frantic thoughts. She wasn't being coddled or pitied. She was being described as a force of nature, an object the sea itself had to reckon with.

The label Lyrra had supplied—*slave, of no account*—shattered. A hot flush of shame rose up her neck. The frantic, buzzing energy in her veins began to settle, replaced by a disorienting calm that seemed to flow not just from the woman's steady gaze, but from the simple, profound truth of her words.

The moment was broken by Lykaon's dry voice from the ship's railing. He raked his gaze over Hanno's soaked, exhausted state.

"Well," he said, a slow smirk spreading across his face. "I've seen you look better. I've also seen you look worse, but that was after three days in a brothel, not a romantic evening swim."

He turned his head slightly, calling over his shoulder. "Kallista, get them some wine. They look like they could use it." He looked back at Hanno and Lyrra. "The cheap stuff," he amended. "No sense wasting the good vintage when they're already half-drowned."

He glanced at the leather pouch still clutched in Hanno's hand. "At least you remembered to bring the rock."

CHAPTER 5
A Pocket of Darkness

The main cabin of Lykaon's ship was a world away from the sun-drenched villa on Issa. It was a spartan, functional space that smelled of salt-cured wood, old rope, and the faint, metallic tang of whetstones. A single lantern, swinging in time with the gentle rock of the sea, cast long, swaying shadows on the walls.

An hour had passed since they'd been hauled from the sea. Kallista had provided them with dry clothes—rough, practical wool that felt strange against Lyrra's skin—and cups of strong, cheap wine that burned a welcome heat in her chest.

The mood was not one of relief, but of heavy, shared exhaustion. Hanno sat on a low bench, brooding, his gaze lost in the depths of his wine cup. Lykaon stood over a chart on the main table, a pragmatic captain plotting a course, his movements efficient and detached.

Lyrra sat between them, a silent observer, the tension between the two men a palpable presence in the small cabin. The only sounds were the steady creak of the ship's timbers and the snap of the sail in the wind outside.

Hanno finally moved, the sound of his bench scraping against the floorboards startlingly loud in the quiet cabin. He needed to ensure their prize was safe. He pulled the heavy, water-stained leather pouch from the pile of their wet clothes and opened it on the table.

The Star of Emesa rolled out. It wasn't a jewel that glittered; it was a piece of polished midnight, a fist-sized, conical meteorite fragment that almost absorbed the lantern light, a pocket of darkness on the table.

Lykaon looked up from his chart. He didn't look at Hanno. His gaze fell on the stone, and his mouth twisted into a thin, bitter line. His voice, when it came, was quiet and dry.

"Going on seven years, and it's still as pretty as that day you chose it over a man's life." His jaw tightened, and he muttered under his breath, a curse swallowed by the creak of the ship's timbers.

Hanno flinched as if he'd been struck. He didn't respond. He just scooped the stone back into its pouch, pulled the drawstring tight with a sharp, angry tug, and shoved it away.

Lykaon watched the motion, his eyes cold. "Just keep it safe," he muttered, more to himself than to Hanno. "Telemon's bounty is the only thing making this partnership tolerable. Barely."

The tension in the room tripled. Lyrra saw the barb land, a direct, brutal hit. She didn't understand the history behind the words, but she understood the language of a well-aimed wound.

The silence that followed was heavier, sharper. It was a weapon now. Kallista entered the cabin, refilled their cups without a word, and retreated, a ghost of quiet empathy in a room thick with unspoken violence.

The hours passed. The ship sailed on into the deep of the night. Hanno drank to numb the past that had just been dragged, bleeding, into the present. His knuckles were white where he gripped the rough clay of his cup. Lykaon drank with the steady, practiced rhythm of a man who lived with ghosts, his focus never straying from his charts for long, but always, eventually, flicking back to Hanno.

Lyrra watched them both, a spectator at a war waged in silence. She saw the storm brewing in Hanno's rigid shoulders, in the tight, angry set of his jaw. She saw the cold, bitter resolve in Lykaon's eyes.

It was Lykaon, his inhibitions finally worn away by the wine, who broke the truce.

"You know, the real joke is that Telemon thinks you're some kind of mastermind," he said, his voice a low, contemptuous drawl. "He doesn't know you're just a coward who got lucky."

That was the spark.

Hanno slammed his cup down on the table. The clay shattered, dark wine splashing across the worn wood like a spray of blood. He was on his feet, his chair crashing backward, his face a mask of raw, cornered fury.

"Coward?" he snarled, the word ripped from his throat. "It wasn't for pride! It was for our future! The one you wanted just as much as I did! It was everything we had!"

Lykaon rose to meet him, moving with a coiled, dangerous grace, his own voice a low snarl, the years of pragmatic detachment burned away to reveal the raw wound beneath. "I ran to save what was left! And you? You got my cousin killed for a bet! For money!"

The accusation hung in the air. *My cousin killed.*

The rage drained from Hanno's face as if a plug had been pulled. It left behind a hollow, gut-punched shock, his eyes suddenly wide with the ghost of a nineteen-year-old boy's horror. The fight was over. He had been defeated not by a fist, but by a memory.

Lyrra felt the air leave her lungs, trapped between them, a spectator to a war that had been raging for seven years. This wasn't a story. This was the unhealed wound of their past, finally torn open. She was witnessing the true, bloody cost of Hanno's legend, and it was a price paid by the dead.

The argument had ended with a bitter silence. Hanno stumbled back a step, his expression shattered, then turned and stalked out of the cabin.

Lyrra found him on the deck, at the stern of the ship. He was staring out at the dark, churning wake, his back to the world, his shoulders hunched as if against a physical weight. The wind whipped short strands of his dark hair across his face, but he didn't seem to notice.

She came up beside him and didn't speak. She just took his hand.

He flinched, a small, sharp motion, and tried to pull away, but she held on, her grip a firm, unwavering connection to the present. For a long moment, they just stood there, her small hand wrapped around his, the silence stretching between them.

"The story everyone tells..." he finally choked out, the words rough, broken. "About the race. My brilliant insight about the pitch ... it's true." He let out a harsh, broken sound that was half laugh, half sob. "But it's not how I knew for certain."

She waited, her eyes fixed on his rigid profile against the dark sea.

"The bet? It was everything we had," he continued, his voice trembling, fragmented. "Every coin Lykaon and I had scraped together. Our entire future. I had my theory … but what if I was wrong? I couldn't— I couldn't let us lose."

His voice cracked, and he stopped. He choked on the memory. Lyrra squeezed his hand. "What did you do, Hanno?" she asked, her voice a soft, steady prompt in the darkness.

"We snuck into the harbor. It was the night before," he finally managed to say, the words a painful admission. "Me, Lykaon, and … and his cousin. Dorian. Just for a look at the hull. Had to be sure. But I was careless … alerted the guards. Got trapped. We had to go into the water."

He stopped, his whole body shuddering with the memory.

"It was so cold … dark. We were separated. When we found each other … he was gone. Dorian. He was gone." He swallowed hard, his gaze fixed on the black water as if seeing it again. "Then we saw them. The guards. Dragging his body from the water … onto the dock." The final words were a hollow sound, swallowed by the wind. "We just … watched."

As he spoke, Lyrra reached up and placed her hand flat on his chest, over his heart. A simple, grounding touch. *I am here. I am not going anywhere.*

"The guards … they were all focused on him," Hanno whispered, his voice shallow. "That was our chance. We just … swam. We used his body as our escape." He finally turned to her, his eyes filled with a seven-year-old agony. "And the next day, I used the certainty that boy died for … and I won the race."

He let out a harsh, bitter laugh that had no humor in it. "Some *brilliance* that was."

She looked at him, at the raw shame twisting his face, and after a long silence, her voice was soft but steady. "That was a terrified boy who made an impossible choice. That boy is not the man holding my hand."

"My whole reputation," he said, shaking his head, the words a raw wound. "It's built on that boy's death."

"No," she countered, her voice gaining strength, refusing to let him fall. "Your reputation is built on everything you did *after*. You survived. You built a life. You found me. *That* is what's real."

"We just left him there, Lyrra." He looked away, unable to meet her eyes. She gently placed a hand on his jaw and turned his face back to hers, forcing him to see the complete lack of judgment in her expression.

"I don't know how to fix this," he said, his voice barely a whisper.

"You don't have to," she said, her own voice an unbreakable promise. "*We* do."

CHAPTER 6
A Sacred Reflection

She left Hanno on the deck, a solitary figure communing with the ghosts of the black water.

Lyrra re-entered the main cabin, the heavy door swinging shut behind her, cutting off the sound of the wind. The air inside was stale, thick with the smell of spilled wine and the bitter tang of old fear. She saw the shattered remains of Hanno's cup on the table, a dark stain spreading into the wood. In the corner, Lykaon was slumped on a bench, a casualty of wine and memory, his head on his chest, a soft snore rumbling from his throat. The silence itself felt loud, a testament to the storm that had just passed.

The adrenaline of the fight and the raw vulnerability of Hanno's confession had left a residue, a restless, pulsing energy under her skin. It was a vibration with nowhere to go, a question her body was asking that she had no answer for. She needed to feel something. Something real. Something that was hers alone.

Kallista was there, a point of calm in the chaos. She moved through the small cabin with a quiet, deliberate grace, collecting the empty wine cups, her movements a silent counterpoint to the raw, jagged emotions that still hung in the air. She didn't look at Lyrra, but Lyrra felt herself being seen. Kallista saw the restless energy, the tension coiled in her shoulders.

Kallista paused her work. She went to a small, dark wood sea chest in the corner, its surface worn smooth by years of travel. She opened it, retrieved a clean, folded piece of linen and a small, polished silver mirror, its surface gleaming like a pool of dark water in the lantern light.

She didn't come to Lyrra. She went to a small, secluded bunk tucked into an alcove, a space that offered a sliver of privacy. She laid the linen down, placed the mirror upon it, and only then did she turn and look at Lyrra.

Her voice was a low, calm alto that quieted the chaos in the room. "When the sea is a storm outside," she said, "a captain cannot command the waves. She can only know her own ship, and trust in its strength."

Kallista offered a small, soft smile, a gesture of pure, uncomplicated empathy. Then, she retreated to the far side of the cabin, turning her back to mend a tear in a sailcloth, giving Lyrra the illusion of privacy, but her presence remained a quiet, supportive anchor in the swaying room.

The invitation was open, but not forced. The polished silver lay on the clean linen, a silent, profound offering. Lyrra looked at the bunk, and her mind went back to Gisco's cold villa. The first time she had claimed her own body, it had been an act of silent, desperate defiance. This... this felt different. Not a rebellion, but an exploration. An invitation.

She made her decision. She crossed the small space and sat on the edge of the secluded bunk.

The overwhelming energy under her skin was still there. She let her hand drift down, her fingers tracing the shape of herself— the soft folds of skin, the delicate structure of her lips. She thought of how they could feel, sometimes, like the dead, barren earth of a desert. And how, with Hanno, or with her own touch, they could become slick and alive, a sudden gush of wetness like rain falling on the sea.

That was the mystery. It wasn't just a physical release. It felt like a connection to something deeper, a source of power that was an extension of herself, but one she didn't know how to name.

She looked over at the still, quiet shape of Kallista across the cabin. Her voice, when it came, was a low, hesitant whisper, barely disturbing the air.

"In Carthage ... when I did this ... I felt a power I'd never known." She paused, searching for the right words. "It's not just pleasure. It feels like ... a part of me I was never told existed. I want to understand it."

Kallista turned, her movements fluid and unhurried. The look in her eyes was one of such profound, gentle empathy that it momentarily stole Lyrra's breath. She crossed the small cabin and came to sit on the floor near the bunk, not too close, but present.

"Then let us look at it together," she said, her voice a low, resonant hum.

Lyrra stared at her, a Roman noblewoman trying to process this radical, shame-free acceptance. "But how... how do you know these things?" she stammered, the question a clumsy attempt to understand the source of Kallista's wisdom. "Were you—"

Kallista's smile was soft, without a trace of bitterness. She finished the thought for her, her voice calm and unapologetic. "A prostitute? Yes. I slept with men for coin—dock workers, merchants, dignitaries." A flash of something knowing and complex entered her eyes. "Women, too."

Lyrra was left speechless, the blunt, simple truth of it shattering the last of her preconceived notions.

"The men who paid for my time," Kallista continued, her voice still a gentle hum, "they didn't just want my body. They wanted a mirror. One that showed them the man they wished they were—powerful, desired, a conqueror. A woman who does not know the truth of her own reflection can only show a man what he wants to see. But a woman who knows her own body, who knows the source of her own power … she can choose what reflection to show. She can shape the man who looks into it."

She picked up the silver mirror. "And that is a power they can never own. It begins here. In seeing yourself without fear."

She held the mirror for Lyrra, angling it.

A cold wave of Roman propriety washed over her—*look away, this is base, this is shameful*—but Kallista's presence was a warm, steadying hand on her back, even from across the small space. Lyrra forced herself to look.

There, in the dark, polished silver, was a reflection of something both alien and intimately familiar. A soft tangle of dark hair, the delicate, complicated pink of her flesh.

"The gate to the temple," Kallista whispered. "Every part of it is sacred."

Lyrra's own hand, which had been resting on her thigh, moved with a new, deliberate curiosity. She touched herself, her eyes fixed on the reflection. She watched as the touch created an immediate reaction. The soft lips plumped, growing fuller, slicker.

A blush, a deep, vibrant pink, spread not just across her cheeks, but across the flesh in the mirror. She let out a small, sharp gasp.

"The heart of the temple is a pearl," Kallista said, her voice a quiet murmur. "Small, but it holds the entire sea."

Lyrra's fingers found it. That small, hard knot of flesh. She circled it gently, and her whole body responded. A low hum started deep in her belly, vibrating through the wood of the bunk beneath her. The scent of her own arousal, musky and female, rose to meet her.

She heard a soft sigh from across the cabin, a breath that was not her own. Lyrra looked up from the mirror. Kallista had leaned her head back against the wall, her eyes closed, a look of serene concentration on her face. Her own hand had disappeared into the folds of her woolen dress.

A slow, secret smile spread across Lyrra's face. This was not a lesson. This was a ritual.

She returned her focus to the mirror, to herself. She began to move her fingers, setting a slow, deliberate rhythm, a silent conversation with her own body. She heard Kallista's breathing quicken, a soft counterpoint to her own.

Faster now. A shared rhythm. Her mind emptied of everything but the building pleasure. The creak of the ship, the faint snoring of the men, the fear of the hunt—all of it faded away, replaced by this. This heat. This focus. This incredible, rising power. Her back arched, her hips pushing against her own hand. The tension gathered in her belly, a focused point of sensation coiling tighter and tighter, a spring wound to the breaking point.

She heard Kallista let out a soft, breathy cry, a sound of pure, uninhibited release. That sound broke the final dam within her.

Her own cry was a feral sound torn from her throat, a nameless, wordless scream. Her whole body went rigid, her inner muscles clenching and pulsing in a violent, shattering rhythm. The pleasure was a shockwave that splintered through her, obliterating every last thread of the frightened Roman girl she had been.

The tremors subsided slowly, leaving a deep, liquid warmth in their wake. Her muscles, which had been coiled tight as bowstrings, went lax. She let her hand fall away, her breath coming in ragged, peaceful gasps. The air in the cabin felt different. Charged and clean.

She slowly lowered the mirror.

Kallista's eyes were open now, and they met Lyrra's across the small space. It was a look of shared knowledge, of a secret understood, and of deep and personal recognition. A foundation had been laid in a language that had no need for words.

CHAPTER 7
The Weighted Chart

Morning light, thin and grey, filtered through the salt-grimed porthole. The air was heavy with the scent of stale wine. Hanno stared into his cup, saying nothing. Across the cabin, Lykaon studied a sea chart, his back to them.

Kallista set a plate of hard bread and dried figs on the table. Lykaon, without turning, grunted, "Just leave it." Hanno reached for a piece of bread, then seemed to think better of it, his hand falling back to his cup.

Lyrra sat between them in the silence. She watched as Kallista moved to her side, offering the plate again, this time just to her. A quiet, supportive gesture. Lyrra took a piece of bread, the simple act feeling like a declaration of allegiance.

Suddenly, a shout came from the deck above. *"Sail to windward!"*

Hanno and Lykaon were on their feet, their personal animosity shed, moving to the nearest porthole together, a synchronized dance of two predators assessing a threat.

"Merchantman," Hanno said, his voice low. "Heading for Crete."

"Flying a crimson banner," Lykaon added, his eyes narrowed. "Roman color. I don't like it. Could be a false-flag patrol."

For a tense minute, the pair watched the ship continue, their shoulders almost touching. Lyrra saw the chasm between them vanish, replaced by solid ground made of their shared expertise and the practical need for survival. The ship continued on its course, oblivious. The threat passed.

The tension did not. They moved back to the table, the shared moment of professionalism evaporated, leaving the awkward silence to settle between them again.

Finally, Lykaon rolled up the chart he'd been studying and unrolled a new one, a larger map of the Adriatic coastline. The dry crackle of the papyrus was loud in the quiet cabin. He weighted the corners with a whetstone and a spare dagger.

"We have nothing. No allies. No clear path." His voice was a flat, pragmatic rasp. "So, what, we keep sailing in circles until they find us? That's no plan. More like a slow death."

He finally looked up, his slate-grey eyes sweeping over both of them, demanding an answer.

"So," he said, his finger tapping the empty sea on the chart. "Where are we going?"

Hanno started to speak, his expression still lost in the fog of the previous night's confession, but Lyrra placed a hand on his arm, a quiet, steadying pressure. Her own mind, in contrast, felt keen, honed by the raw honesty of the last twelve hours—incisive. She leaned forward, eyes fixed on the map.

"We can't go to any major Roman or Greek ports," she said, her voice even and sure. "And we can't hide on a small island; we've seen how quickly that becomes a trap."

She looked up, meeting Lykaon's appraising stare without flinching.

"We need a place that is large enough to disappear in, but chaotic enough that no one asks questions. A place where allegiances are cheap and information is for sale."

Hanno looked up from his cup, his focus shifting from the dark wine to her. As she spoke, laying out the parameters of their survival, his eyes sharpened, the fog of memory burning away, replaced by the familiar intensity of the strategist. Pride and confidence pierced through the lingering haze of his confession. He leaned over the chart, his finger tracing the rugged Illyrian coastline.

His finger stopped on a large, dark island.

"Korkyra," he said, his voice regaining its familiar, confident edge. "It's a crossroads. Greek colonists on the coast, Illyrian pirates in the hills, Roman traders who pay them both off. Everyone goes there, and no one trusts anyone else." He looked up, a grim smile touching his lips. "It's a viper's nest."

Lykaon studied the chart for a long moment, then gave a single, curt nod of approval.

"A viper's nest," he said, a flash of his dry wit returning, "is the perfect place to hide from vultures."

CHAPTER 8
Skeletal Hill

They sailed for two days, a tense, silent journey south through the Adriatic. The ship became a small, self-contained world defined by Hanno's brooding silence and Lykaon's pointed avoidance. Lyrra learned the rhythm of the sea, the creak of the rigging, the snap of the sail, while the two men circled each other like wary predators.

They arrived at Korkyra under the cover of a pre-dawn mist, the island a massive, pine-bristled spine against a grey sky. This was no backwater. Even in the dim light, Lyrra could see the formidable stone walls of a true city, the silhouettes of dozens of ships crowding a harbor that was already a tangle of competing traffic.

As they glided toward the docks, the full, chaotic character of the place revealed itself. Lean, hard-faced Illyrian pirates, their skin tanned to the color of old leather, haggled over stolen goods with shrewd Greek traders. The air was thick with the smells of pine tar, roasting fish, and cheap, sour wine. It was a city that thrived on the edge of a dozen different laws.

Then she saw them.

A group of five men swaggered down the main thoroughfare, parting the crowd not with politeness, but with the sheer, brutal confidence of apex predators. One of them, a hulking brute with a chipped tooth, casually shoved a fruit vendor's cart aside, sending oranges scattering across the cobblestones, and didn't even glance back. They weren't dressed like the local pirates or the typical

Greek sailors. They wore mismatched pieces of heavy armor, their swords worn with a casual, deadly familiarity. Their faces were hard, etched with cruel lines, their eyes constantly moving, assessing everything and everyone for weakness. There was a disciplined ferocity about them, a feral energy that felt utterly out of place.

"Cowshit," Lykaon cursed, his voice a low, grim sound from beside her.

Lyrra looked at him, her stomach dropping. "What ... Romans?"

"Worse than Romans," he said, his eyes narrowed. "They call themselves the Mamertines—'Sons of Mars.' Campanian mercenaries. Agathocles's old dogs from Syracuse. They decided they liked pillaging more than taking orders. Completely amoral."

The viper's nest had vipers of its own.

They docked the ship in a crowded, anonymous slip, far from the main berths. Hanno and Lyrra were to remain on board, out of sight, while Lykaon went to ground.

"You two have faces that are becoming expensive," he'd said with his usual dry wit before disappearing into the morning mist. "Mine just looks like every other ugly bastard in a port like this. Stay here. I'll go listen to the whispers."

He was gone for hours. Lyrra and Hanno waited in the tense silence of the cabin. The idea of being hunted was a physical pressure compressing the walls around them. When Lykaon finally returned, his face was grim, stripped of its usual cynical humor. He dropped a loaf of bread and a skin of wine on the table.

"It's worse than I thought," he said. He looked at Hanno. "There are at least a handful of the bounty men Telemon hired on the island. Asking questions in every tavern and brothel. Clumsy, but loud."

He paused, his expression darkening. "And he's brought in professionals. I hear there's a military man—Roman— leading those Mamertines that we spotted. He's asking questions, too. Seems Telemon is sparing no expense."

Hanno swore under his breath, a low, vicious sound. "Melqart's hells, has he hired every cutthroat from here to Sicily? That man never understood subtlety."

Lyrra watched him, saw the way he clenched his fists, the raw frustration of a commander forced to be passive. She realized he was deliberately deferring to Lykaon. This was not Hanno's world of calculated trade and high-stakes wagers; this was Lykaon's world of back-alley whispers and mercenary codes. It wasn't weakness; it was the cold, hard strategy of a leader letting his specialist take the lead.

"Looks that way," Lykaon confirmed. "The city is crawling with them. We're not safe here."

The final piece of the puzzle seemed to slam into place. Telemon's hunt was more extensive and more dangerous than they had ever imagined. They were not just being pursued; they were being systematically cornered.

"The city is a trap," Hanno said, his voice a low, grim echo of Lykaon's assessment. "We can't stay on the ship, and we can't be seen in the port."

"Then we go to ground," Lykaon said, already moving, his mind all pragmatic efficiency. "Somewhere high. Defensible. Where we can see them coming."

They left the ship under the cover of the deepening twilight, moving one by one, shadows slipping through the chaotic energy of the docks. They followed a steep, goat-track of a path that wound its way up from the city and into the dark, pine-scented hills that loomed over the port.

The climb was arduous, the air growing cooler as they ascended. Kallista, moving with her usual quiet grace, paused to pluck a cluster of dark berries from a thorny bush, tucking them into a fold of her dress with a knowing, economical movement. A small, silent nod to her own unique expertise. At one point, the path narrowed over a treacherous patch of loose shale. Lykaon, in the lead, navigated it with practiced ease. Hanno, following, instinctively reached back, his hand finding Lykaon's arm to steady him over a loose rock—a moment of professional muscle memory that bypassed seven years of bitterness. Lykaon didn't acknowledge the touch, but he didn't pull away. For a single, shared beat, they were not rivals; they were soldiers on the same desperate retreat.

Lyrra felt the burn in her calves, the ache in her lungs, and a strange, grim satisfaction. Every ache was proof that the soft Roman noblewoman was being left behind, something harder taking her place. The innocent little girl who once feared the loud *bang* of a dropped crate now felt a sharpening of her own senses, a quickening of her mind in this brutal landscape. This world, for all its danger, was making her truly alive.

Finally, Lykaon led them to their destination: the skeletal ruins of an old farmhouse, perched on a cliffside overlooking the sea. The roof was long gone, the stone walls crumbling, but it offered a commanding view of the harbor below and the single path that led up to it. It was a discreet, defensible position.

As the last of the light faded from the sky, they settled into the ruins, the four of them a small, isolated pocket of humanity in the vast, silent darkness. Below them, the lights of Korkyra glittered, the beautiful, treacherous fires of the mercenaries that held them under siege. Every light was a potential enemy.

Lyrra scanned the harbor. A new ship, dark and fast, had just slipped into the main berth, its silhouette another cold nail in their coffin. They were hidden—for now—but they were trapped on the island, surrounded by hunters who were still dangerously unknown.

CHAPTER 9
A Rain of Stone

The skeletal ruins of the old farmhouse, perched high on the cliffs of Korkyra, had become their temporary sanctuary. The roof was long gone, but the crumbling stone walls offered shelter from the wind, and the commanding view of the harbor below was their most valuable asset.

It was late morning the next day. The sun, already high, beat down on the hills with a heavy, golden warmth. They had fallen into a rough, efficient routine. Kallista, a point of quiet industry, sat near a patch of sunlight, mending a tear in Lykaon's tunic with deft fingers. Hanno and Lykaon took turns on watch, scanning the winding path that led up from the city and the distant, sparkling expanse of the harbor.

"Still nothing but fat merchants and bored guards," Lykaon muttered, his cynical gaze sweeping the docks. "Telemon's vultures are either blind or drunk. Probably both."

Hanno's jaw remained tight, his stare on the harbor unwavering. "They're not known for their patience," he said, his voice flat, a grim assessment. "But they're here. Somewhere."

Kallista didn't look up, her voice a low, philosophical murmur. "Even a blind man can stumble upon a treasure if he walks long enough."

Lyrra, meanwhile, was practicing her dagger, her movements growing more fluid, more confident with each passing hour. The steel was a familiar weight in her hand, an instrument of her will.

She felt the quiet satisfaction of their temporary safety, the sun warm on her skin, the wind cool in her hair. She was learning to use her dagger, to observe, to anticipate. She was ready for the next challenge.

Kallista's final stitch was as precise as her first. She knotted the thread, snipped it, and carefully wrapped up the remaining thread, stashing the small sewing materials away into a drawstring pouch. She held up the tunic, shook it once, and folded it nicely.

Lyrra moved to the harbor side of the ruins alongside Hanno. Her eyes, like Hanno's, now swept the harbor. A small, fast trireme was cutting through the morning chop, heading for the main docks. *More hunters*, she thought, a moment of grim recognition. *One of Lykaon's clumsy vultures. Certainly they'll come up the path.*

The quiet was shattered by the sudden, sharp crack of a large stone falling on the pebble and dirt path below that led toward the sea.

Hanno and Lykaon moved as one, their bodies tensing, their hands going to their weapons. "Mercenaries," Hanno muttered, his voice grim, already anticipating the uncoordinated rush of Telemon's men from the entryway.

No men came through.

A hail of rocks, heavy and jagged, rained down from the crumbling walls of the farmhouse itself, followed by the terrifying, guttural roar of men. The attack came from above. They were already inside.

Across the ruins, Kallista moved with a fluid silence, melting into the deep shadows of a crumbling wall, her eyes wide but her movements deliberate. Once out of sight, her eyes narrowed with a sharp, assessing focus.

Lyrra spun, her dagger instinctively flashing into her hand. The air filled with the stench of stale sweat and old blood—the same scent she had noticed in the market. Five figures, clad in mismatched armor, dropped from the higher sections of the ruins, moving with a disciplined ferocity that was utterly unlike the disorganized chaos of a bounty hunter. These were not Telemon's vultures.

These were Mamertines.

The ruins erupted in a clash of steel and shouts. Hanno and Lykaon, expecting the wild, disorganized rush of Telemon's men, met the attack with their own brutal efficiency. Hanno's short sword was a blur, deflecting a blow, then driving forward with a guttural roar. Lykaon, retrieving his own blade, moved with a cynical grace, his movements economical, deadly.

But the Mamertines ignored them.

Their focus was absolute, terrifyingly precise. Two of them engaged Hanno, their heavy shields locking him in a brutal dance of deflection and parry. Another two moved with chilling speed to cut off Lykaon, their swords clanging against his, forcing him back, away from Lyrra.

Lyrra, her dagger still clutched in her hand, suddenly found herself exposed. She had expected to fight beside Hanno, to be a small, sharp point of defense in their united front. Instead, a fifth Mamertine, a hulking brute with a scarred face, detached himself from the main fight and moved directly toward her. His eyes, cold and dead, were fixed solely on her.

The air vibrated with the clang of steel, the grunts of men, the potent smell of dust and fear. Lyrra tasted the metallic tang of adrenaline on her tongue. The hulking Mamertine lunged, his scarred face a mask of brutal intent. Lyrra met him, her dagger lashing out, but his heavy shield took the blow with a dull *thud*. He swatted her to the side like a fly, his hand reaching for her, to seize her.

"Lyrra!" Hanno roared, his voice a guttural sound of pure, unadulterated terror. He saw it then—the Mamertines weren't fighting him. They were *holding* him. Pinning him in place while their compeer went for her. He slammed his elbow back, catching one of his attackers in the jaw, sending him stumbling, but another immediately took his place.

Lykaon, too, saw the shift. "They want the girl!" he yelled, his voice raw with horrifying understanding. He tried to break free, his movements desperate, but the two Mamertines holding him were disciplined, relentless.

Amidst the chaos, Lyrra saw Kallista move, keeping low, creeping along the perimeter towards the back. She carefully slipped through a deep gap in the rear wall like a silent shadow, vanishing from the brawl. Lyrra felt a pang of fear—*abandonment*—but then she saw Kallista's face reappear, only her eyes visible. Her expression was one of intense concentration, while her eyes scanned the crumbling ruins: the masonry, the patches of loose scree, the integrity of the walls.

The halfwalls of stone echoed with grunts and the sickening clang of steel, and Lyrra was the desperate, defiant center of it all, dodging, weaving, her dagger a flash of silver as she tried to keep the hulking Mamertine at bay. His heavy hands grabbed, snatched at her, his movements surprisingly agile for his size. She could feel the wind of his blows, the brush of his calloused fingers against her tunic.

Hanno fought with a desperate, animalistic fury, roaring curses, his eyes fixed on Lyrra. He was trapped, forced to watch.

Lyrra parried a clumsy swing, her arm jarring from the impact. Kallista looked over to Lyrra, who was trapped by the brute. For a moment, Lyrra caught a glimpse of Kallista's scrutinizing eyes from across the ruins, locked on the wall behind Lyrra.

The hulking Mamertine had Lyrra cornered against a crumbling section of wall. His heavy shield slammed against the stone, pinning her. He reached for her, his rough fingers closing tight on the wool of her tunic.

Kallista gave a sharp, decisive nod. Then she was gone, disappearing around the crumbling stonework toward the harbor side.

Then, a commanding, precise voice cut through the din of battle. A voice that carried the weight of tactical authority, utterly out of place in this feral chaos.

A large man with the calm, disciplined look of a Roman legionary stepped out from behind a crumbling archway. He moved forward, his crimson cloak billowing slightly behind him, his eyes, flat and devoid of emotion, fixed on Lyrra.

"Leave the men," he commanded, his voice hard and purposeful. "Secure the girl."

CHAPTER 10
The Death of a Name

"Yes, Decimus, sir," grunted the hulking Mamertine as he released Lyrra, his grip instantly replaced by Decimus's own. His fingers, surprisingly soft yet firm, closed around her arm, pulling her away from the crumbling wall. He moved with the economical precision of a Roman soldier. He held her at arm's length, appraising her with a cool sweep of his eyes. She felt the familiar prickle of being property, but this time, it was laced with a chilling, personal malice.

"Lady Aemilia," Decimus said, his voice a low, condescending murmur, tailored for a frightened, docile noblewoman.

That name. The one she burned away.

"Your father has gone to considerable expense for your return. Do not make this difficult."

He smiled then, a thin, humorless twist of his lips that was utterly devoid of warmth. He saw a runaway girl, a disgraced patrician. He saw weakness. He saw a prize. His hand, the one not holding her arm, moved toward her face, intending to cup her cheek, to assert his easy dominance.

It was the precise moment Lyrra had been waiting for.

She didn't flinch. She didn't scream. Her own hand had been resting casually at her side. Now it moved with a speed that defied the eye. The dagger, a cold, familiar weight, flashed from its sheath.

Decimus, caught completely off-guard by her audacity, instinctively threw up his hand to block, a reflex born of years in the legion.

The point slid through the thick muscle of his palm, pinning his hand to the air. Decimus roared—a raw, animal sound that shattered his cold Roman composure entirely. For a heartbeat, he was just a man in pain, staring in disbelief at the blade pinning his hand. Then his training reasserted itself. His eyes, still wide with shock, locked onto hers with a new, grudging assessment.

Lyrra leaned in close, her breath hot against his ear, her voice no longer a whisper, but a cold, clear hiss. "Tell my father," she snarled, twisting the hilt of the dagger, "his property 'Lady Aemilia' is dead."

The pain in his eyes sharpened, but beneath it, Lyrra saw a spark of something else—a dawning, horrified respect. He tried to pull away, but the blade held him fast.

She yanked the dagger free with a brutal, sickening tear of flesh, the blade slick with his blood. Decimus stumbled back, clutching his ruined hand, his face pale with shock and fury.

"Your father..." he choked out, his voice raw with pain. His eyes were fixed on Lyrra, taking in his disastrous miscalculation. "...he doesn't pay enough for this. To return a, what... what I can only guess is a fellow mercenary?"

"You should tell your friends that. Save face." Hanno's voice jabbed from where he was pinned across the ruins.

Lykaon barked a laugh, his voice cutting through the grunts of the two men holding him. "Better yet, tell 'em *he* was *seven* feet tall!"

The Mamertine holding him grunted, his grip tightening in a silent warning.

Decimus pressed harder on his hand, grinding a wince away with his teeth. "And your father paid better than what that cheap Carthaginian bitch offered. And she wanted you brought back in pieces."

The words slammed into Lyrra, a cold, brutal shock that made her stomach clench. Sybil. She hadn't forgotten. She had tried to hire Decimus, too.

Hanno's eyes were fixed on Lyrra—the dagger, the blood, the defiant fury in her eyes. His focus shifted for a barest second to something over her shoulder—a familiar flash of movement from beyond the wall—and a new, fierce urgency hardened his expression.

"Go!" Hanno yelled, his voice desperate. "Now!"

The stillness shattered with Hanno's roar. He had finally broken free of the Mamertines, his short sword a blur of motion. Lykaon, too, was fighting with renewed ferocity, his eyes fixed on the path to freedom.

Hanno and Lykaon became a furious wall of muscle, pushing a path through the Mamertines to the entryway. Lyrra didn't hesitate. She turned to follow them, but her path to the main entryway was cut off by Decimus and the hulking Mamertine.

Just as Decimus lunged for her, a hand shot out from a narrow gap in the crumbling wall just behind her, grabbing her arm. It was Kallista, breathing hard but focused. Her face was pale but her eyes blazing with fierce urgency. She had slipped through a dark, narrow gap in the stone wall a few feet behind Lyrra.

"This way!" she hissed, her voice a sharp command.

She pulled Lyrra through the opening and into the open air on the hillside overlooking the sea. They scrambled over loose shale and thorny bushes, the sounds of the fight fading slightly behind them. Ahead, Lyrra could see the main path winding down the hill—their only route to safety.

As they emerged from the scrub onto the path, she looked up just in time to see Hanno and Lykaon burst from the ruins' main entryway. For a heart-stopping second, it looked like a clean break.

Decimus looked from his bleeding hand to his men struggling against the renewed fury of their opponents. His eyes shifted to Lyrra, now a liability. The calculation was instant. He raised his good hand, his voice sharp cutting through the din. "Stand down! Let them go."

His command came a fraction too late. One Mamertine, the hulking brute who had first cornered Lyrra, ignored the order in a final, frustrated lunge at the closest target—Lykaon, who was covering their retreat.

Lykaon spun to meet the attack, parrying the main thrust, but the man's sheer, brutish force drove the parry wide, the steel biting deep into his left forearm. A sharp, guttural grunt was torn from Lykaon's throat.

"Lykaon!" Hanno's cry was raw. He didn't hesitate, spinning back to grab Lykaon's good arm, half-dragging him down the path toward Lyrra and Kallista.

Lyrra watched them come, her heart hammering against her ribs. She saw dark blood already dripping onto the stones of the path, a new, terrible price for their escape.

The sounds of battle faded behind them as they scrambled down a steep, rocky path. Lyrra risked a final glance back. Decimus was watching them with the cold stare of a general who had just learned a painful lesson. He had made a tactical retreat, cutting his losses rather than risk his men for inadequate coin. But in his eyes, she saw a promise: the next time they met, he would come prepared for the right war.

CHAPTER 11

The Turn of the Tide

They scrambled into the mouth of a small, hidden cave along the Korkyran coast, their bodies aching, their lungs burning. The sounds of pursuit, the distant shouts and clang of steel, slowly faded behind them, swallowed by the roar of the sea. The air inside was damp, cool, and smelled of salt and wet stone.

Hanno and Lykaon immediately moved to the cave's entrance, their faces grim, scanning the twilight for any sign of their pursuers. Kallista knelt beside a small pool of freshwater, dipping a piece of linen to tend to their injuries in the dim light.

Kallista moved to Lykaon, her practiced hands examining the gash on his left forearm. The wound was clean but deep enough to need attention.

"Hold still," she murmured, tearing a strip of clean, damp linen. "It should heal without hampering your sword work, but it will need proper binding to prevent infection." Lykaon winced as she wrapped it tight, but his fingers flexed normally when she finished. "It'll hold," she said with quiet satisfaction.

Lyrra sank onto a patch of dry stone, the dull throb in her thigh where the Mamertine had almost caught her a constant reminder. The image of Decimus's bleeding hand, and his chilling words— *He pays better than that Carthaginian bitch*—replayed in her mind. Her father. Sybil. And Telemon, still out there, wanting his stone and his pound of flesh. Three separate, relentless predators, each with their own motive.

Sybil, Lyrra thought, a cold, bitter amusement fleeting through her fear. Asha's words, sharp and crude, echoed in her mind: *Just an asshole doing asshole things.* She let out a little huff.

The weight of this new, triple threat was immense, a pressure that seemed to shrink the very walls of the cave.

Hanno paced the cramped space, his shoulders tight with a coiled anger, his frustration a low, dangerous hum. He wasn't just furious at the hunters; he was furious at himself. For being caught off guard. For letting Lyrra be exposed. For the momentary lapse in vigilance that had brought his two worlds crashing down.

The silence in the cave grew heavy, punctuated only by the distant roar of the sea and the soft drip of water from the stalactites. Hanno flinched at a sudden, sharp crack from outside—a branch snapping in the wind—his hand going to his sword hilt. Lyrra found herself constantly scanning the cave mouth, even though she knew it was futile, her eyes darting from shadow to shadow. Every gust of wind carried the whisper of pursuit. They were cornered, trapped on an island that had suddenly become too small.

Hanno stopped pacing, his gaze sweeping over Lykaon's grim face, then Kallista's quiet calm, and finally, Lyrra's determined expression. "We can't keep running forever," he said, his voice raw with frustration. "They'll catch up at some point. We're bleeding time and resources."

Lyrra looked at the map Lykaon had unrolled earlier, still lying on the stone floor. Defense would be a closing cage. Running was a slow death. Her eyes fell on the distant, familiar shape of Thera.

A reckless thought took hold, sharp and sudden as her dagger's strike.

She pushed herself up from the stone, her movement decisive, her earlier fear hardened into cold resolve. She stepped into the cramped space between the two men.

"Then we stop running," she declared. "We can't win a war on two fronts. We have to eliminate one threat permanently." With a single, firm press on the shaded shape of an island, she looked up, meeting Hanno's startled face to Lykaon's narrowed eyes. "We go to Thera."

Hanno stared at her, his frustration momentarily forgotten, replaced by a flash of awe. Lykaon, ever pragmatic, studied her, a slow, grudging respect dawning in his face.

CHAPTER 12
Leverage and Lies

The decision to go to Thera hung in the air, a fragile, desperate hope. But hope didn't charter ships. They had a destination, but no vessel, and in a port like Korkyra, a known name like Lykaon's, or a wanted one like Hanno's, was a liability.

They moved through the shadowy corners of the port as dusk settled, the air smelling of brine and squalor. Korkyra was certainly a viper's nest. A haven for pirates and smugglers, but also under the watchful eye of a newly appointed Roman governor, whose legions were a constant, unsettling presence. It was a place where allegiances were a commodity, sold to the highest bidder, and secrets were the currency.

Lykaon, with his network of underworld contacts, led them to a grimy tavern tucked away in a labyrinth of warehouses. The air was thick with greasy smoke from a poorly vented cookfire and the sweat of unwashed men. Every breath felt second-hand. A man sat hunched over a table in the darkest corner. His face was scarred, and a single gold tooth glinted in the gloom when his lips twisted into a smile. His eyes were chips of obsidian. Captain Phormion. A smuggler. A man who would trade his own mother for the right price.

"He'll get us there," Lykaon muttered, his voice low. "But he'll flay us for the coin."

The negotiation was a tense, procedural dance. Lykaon, with his usual blend of cynicism and pragmatism, opened. Hanno stood behind them, a silent, intimidating presence, his hand resting casually on the hilt of his short sword, ensuring they weren't cheated outright.

Phormion, his eyes constantly darting, named an exorbitant price for passage to Thera. Kallista, cool and unflappable, began to negotiate him down, her voice a soft, steady counterpoint to his bluster.

She argued every point, every fee, until only one remained between them: Phormion's insistence on a steep, non-negotiable "hazard payment" for transporting a wanted man.

Lykaon leaned over to Hanno, his whisper a low, dry rasp. "For that price," he muttered, "I'd expect him to not only get us there but to personally carry the lady on his back and fellate us both upon arrival. And I'm not even sure it's worth it then."

A familiar heat, a flash of the old Roman anger, tightened in Lyrra's chest at Lykaon's lewdness. But then she watched Kallista.

With a sigh of theatrical defeat, Kallista seemed to give in on the higher hazard fee, letting Phormion puff out his chest with pride. He turned and barked a sharp command to his crew, all business now that terms were set. He was so focused on his own ego, so convinced of his victory on that final point, that he failed to realize that in arguing for that steep *symbolic fee*, he had conceded far more on the much larger base price. She had handed him a victory to feed his pride, and in exchange, he had unknowingly lowered his guard—and with it, the final cost.

As they rose to leave, the smuggler captain's gaze lingered on Lyrra, a slow, appraising look devoid of respect. "She's a pretty one," Phormion said, his voice thick with insinuation. "What's a

Roman lady doing with two dogs like you? Must be worth a fortune."

Hanno's hand, which had been resting on Lyrra's back, clenched. His eyes, cold as slate, locked onto Phormion's. The easygoing merchant was gone, and a powerful stillness settled over him. "She's my partner," Hanno said, his voice a low, dangerous growl that promised swift, brutal consequences if the man continued. "And she's worth more than your entire fleet. Keep your eyes on your charts, Captain."

Phormion's smirk faltered. He saw the cold fury in Hanno's eyes, and the glint of steel in Lykaon's. He gave a curt, nervous nod. "As you say, merchant."

They left the tavern, the deal secured, but the air was still thick with unspoken threats. Hanno walked with his hand resting on the hilt of his sword, his eyes sweeping the shadowy alleys. Lykaon muttered curses under his breath about the price.

Lyrra, however, was focused on something else entirely. She needed to understand Kallista's method.

They boarded the small, anonymous cargo vessel Phormion had provided, its deck worn smooth by years of hauling illicit goods. Lykaon immediately went to check the rigging, while Hanno scanned the surrounding docks. Kallista, with her usual quiet efficiency, found a secluded spot near the stern and began unpacking a small satchel of provisions.

Lyrra went to her, her voice a low murmur. "Why did you let him have that hazard fee?" She cut straight to the heart of what she had just seen. "The price was so high ... you gave in too easily."

Kallista looked up, her eyes, deep and knowing, meeting Lyrra's. She offered a piece of dried fruit. "His greed was a wall," she said, her voice a soft, philosophical hum. "And I had no hammer to break it. But his pride was a door." She watched Lyrra, a subtle smile touching her lips. "Step back to observe the entire situation. I saw what he truly wanted and gave it to him. In his eyes, *he won*." She paused, watching a gull wheel over the harbor. "His ego blinded him and it cost him coin in the end."

Lyrra stared at her. It wasn't about confrontation. It was about reading the man, finding his core desire, his blindspots, and manipulating it. A cold, sharp clarity settled in Lyrra's mind. She had just witnessed a masterclass.

CHAPTER 13
A Shared Rhythm

The anonymous cargo vessel, Phormion at the helm, cut through the dark waters, leaving the treacherous lights of Korkyra behind. The initial tension of departure, the fear of being spotted, slowly settled into the weary rhythm of the open sea. Lykaon, grim-faced but efficient, took the helm, his gaze fixed on the endless horizon. Below deck, Hanno disappeared to check their meager supplies, while Kallista sat mending a torn sailcloth with quiet concentration.

Lyrra stood on deck, feeling the vastness of the sea, the cool spray on her face. The air was clean here, scrubbed of the port's grime, but the quiet hum of the ship was now laced with the knowledge of unseen threats.

Phormion, a man of few words, led them below deck to their quarters for the night. It was a commandeered cargo bay, small and cramped. It smelled of brine, old wood, and the faint sweetness of dried fruit. Makeshift beds lined the walls—crates covered with scratchy woolen blankets. It was a temporary, improvised space that offered some privacy from the crew. The muffled sounds of sailors drinking and laughing were already filtering through the thin walls.

"Best I can do for now," Phormion grunted, his eyes darting. "We'll offload some cargo and crew at the next port, Zakynthos. Should free up something more ... private for the rest of the journey to Thera."

Lyrra felt the exhaustion in her bones, the weight of the last few days of travel and conflict pressing down on her. But as she looked at the cramped, temporary space, she knew it would be enough. For tonight.

o   o   o   o   o

Hours later, the cargo bay had plunged into near darkness. The single lantern in the passageway outside cast only a faint glow through the cracks in the door. It swayed with the ship's motion, painting the makeshift beds in shifting shadows. Lykaon was already a loud, rhythmic presence in the corner, his snores a distant, rumbling storm. Kallista lay perfectly still in her own makeshift bed, eyes closed, her breathing shallow and even, a picture of serene sleep.

But the ship was far from silent. The sounds of sailors drinking and laughing filtered through the thin wooden walls. Shouts, clattering cups, and bursts of song created a rhythmic, ambient cover.

Lyrra lay spooning with Hanno, her back pressed against his front, facing away from the wall, toward the other makeshift bed. They were both utterly exhausted, the last few days of flight and confrontation having drained them to the bone. Her muscles ached, and the rhythmic sway of the ship was pulling her into a deep, heavy sleep.

Then she felt it.

A subtle, familiar shift in the hard, warm body pressed against her. The slow, insistent hardening of his erection against her backside. A warmth, a thrill, a deep connection that bypassed thought and went straight to her core. Her own body, despite its exhaustion, hummed in immediate response.

The hum in her body intensified, resonating against him, a solid, warm wall behind her growing, stretching, pressing.

She responded instinctively. A gentle, deliberate grind of her backside against him. A slow, deliberate push. *Here. Like this.* Her hips moved, just a fraction, testing the boundary, inviting him deeper into the unspoken language they shared.

She felt his immediate response. A deep groan rumbled from his chest, vibrating through her spine. His arms tightened around her, pulling her back against him. He spooned her closer until there was no space left between them. His hips pressed forward, an answering counter-push, mirroring her unspoken plea.

A fierce wave of pleasure was already building. A slow, building burn, starting low in her belly and spreading, a liquid heat. Her skin prickled. Every nerve ending in her backside, where his cock was now a hard, unyielding presence, came alive. She was testing the boundaries, yes, but she was also reveling in the power of her own body, of her own desire. The tension of the day, the fear of the hunt—it was all beginning to dissolve, melting into this primal, insistent need. This was a different kind of freedom. This was hers.

Hanno's hand, which had been clutching her waist, slid lower, finding the hem of his simple linen undergarment. A slow, deliberate tug. She felt the fabric give, the coarse linen sliding down his thighs, freeing him. His cock, already a thick, insistent presence against her, was now fully exposed, hot, its tip slick against her bare skin.

The audacity of this thrilled her.

Her own hand found the hem of her undergarment. She pulled it aside, the rough wool scraping against her inner thigh, exposing her sex to him, to the dark, to the shared secret. Her lips, already parted, felt suddenly swollen, wet.

He leaned in, his breath hot against her ear. "Really?" he whispered, the word raw with disbelief. "Here?"

Her body was already arching, pushing back against him with a primal need. "Mm-hmm," she fired back, her voice vibrating through her. *Yes. Here. Now. Always.*

Just then, a sudden, loud burst of laughter erupted from the nearby sailors' quarters. A clatter of cups, a heavy thump against the wall. It was jarring, violent, shattering the fragile intimacy of their moment.

They froze.

Lyrra's breath hitched. Her heart hammered against her ribs, a frantic drum against his chest. She could feel his own heart, a frantic, wild thing, beating in time with hers. Motionless. Silent. Listening. The sounds from next door, once a comforting cover, were now a terrifying threat. The air in the cramped cargo bay seemed to thicken, pressing in on them, amplifying every creak of the ship, every distant shout. The risk was immense. The thrill, intoxicating.

The noise from next door faded, leaving a ringing silence in its wake. They waited, motionless, their breaths held, listening. Only the creak of the ship and the distant slap of waves against the hull. The danger, for now, had passed.

They resumed, slow, intentional, careful. Hanno slid his hard, hot cock between her thighs, not quite inside, just pressing against the slick, wet entrance of her vagina. The friction was exquisite, a slow, building burn. Lyrra leaned forward slightly, adjusting her hips, providing a better, deeper angle for his entry into her wet core, her muscles already clenching in anticipation. It was slow, a little awkward, this dance of finding the perfect fit, but deeply, profoundly sensual.

She closed her eyes, letting the pure sensation consume her. The rhythmic sway of the ship, the distant shouts, the feel of Hanno's heated skin against hers, the rough hair of his thighs brushing her own. Her lips parted, a soft moan escaping, swallowed by the darkness. His breath hitched against her neck.

In the throes of the subdued experience, a tremor ran through her. Her eyes fluttered open.

Across the dark cargo bay, in the faint residual light from the distant lantern, she saw Kallista. Her eyes were open. They shone, reflecting the subtle light from under the door.

Lyrra's movements faltered, almost pausing. The world narrowed to that single, piercing gaze.

Hanno didn't stop, lost in the moment. He pushed, a slow, rhythmic grind, the friction of his cock pressed against her, his breath warm against her neck. His hips bucked, a silent plea for more.

Kallista's eyes met Lyrra's. And then, subtle, almost imperceptible in the dim light, Kallista's hand moved. A specific gesture. Her fingers curled, a grabbing motion, pulling them close to her, then pointing at Hanno, repeating the motion.

Lyrra understood. It was a command, a permission, a lesson. *Grab him. Pull him in. Take what you want.*

Her hand moved from her thigh with sudden, fierce purpose. She grabbed Hanno's hip. Her fingers dug into the firm muscle. She pulled. Hard. A desperate tug. She pushed her own body back, grinding him deeper, tighter, against her, a demanding invitation.

A new surge of pleasure, sharp and overwhelming, shot through her. The friction, the heat. The risk of being caught.

Hanno responded instantly. A guttural groan tore from his throat, muffled against her hair. He sped up, his thrusts deeper, more frantic, into a wild rhythm. He was lost. Utterly lost.

Lyrra closed her eyes, her head falling back. Her mind emptied, lost to the raw sensation: the pounding staccato rhythm of him, the feel of his cock stretching her, filling her, pressing her deeper. Her muscles clenched, pulling, milking him. The pleasure coiled tighter, tighter, a spring wound to its absolute breaking point.

She felt him tense, his body signaling his approaching release, which triggered her own. A deep, internal clench. A spark catching tinder in the dark. A stolen fire, hot and fast, that consumed them both in a silent, searing pulse. His name was a choked cry that stuck in her mouth. He poured himself into her, a pulsing flood that filled her completely.

Her own release was a silent scream against his mouth, her muscles contracting over and over again, pulling him deeper, squeezing, milking him dry. Her eyes squeezed shut, lost in the white-hot current. A shared, secret inferno that left them breathless and glowing in the dark.

Hanno fell lifeless against her, his forehead pressed into her hair, his breath ragged against her neck. She could feel him softening inside her, the last pulses of warmth. His body had been taut with need. Now it felt utterly spent, heavy and still.

Lyrra's eyes fluttered open, still dazed, and found Kallista's. This time, Kallista's eyes were closed, her face serene in the dim light, a picture of deep, untroubled sleep. *She's feigning*, Lyrra thought, a slow, secret smile touching her lips.

Just then, a sudden, loud crash of bottles erupted from the crew's quarters next door, followed by a burst of drunken shouts. Lykaon coughed, a rough, hoarse sound, and stirred in his bunk, his snores momentarily interrupted.

Kallista's eyes opened. They met Lyrra's across the dark cargo bay, a shared secret, a silent affirmation passing between them. Then, with a fluid, almost imperceptible movement, Kallista turned over, pulling a blanket higher, and subtly reached out to pat Lykaon's shoulder, a soft, comforting gesture that seemed to lull him back into his heavy sleep.

Lyrra and Hanno were left in their post-coital warmth in the cramped space. Lyrra reached for a clean linen on the crate beside them, and balled it up and slid it up between her legs. Hanno, utterly spent, his body heavy and relaxed, fell asleep almost instantly, his breathing deep and even against her neck.

Lyrra lay awake for a while, her mind stirring, processing the shared intimacy, the quiet guidance, the profound connection. The sounds of the ship, the distant crew, the soft creak of the timbers—it was all part of this new, complex sanctuary. Then, she too drifted off to sleep, a deep, satisfied slumber.

CHAPTER 14

Lesson in Logistics

Lyrra woke slowly, wrapped in the warmth of Hanno's arms, her head tucked into the curve of his shoulder. The exhaustion that had been in her yesterday had been replaced by a deep, languid peace.

Hanno stirred beside her, his first waking expression a soft, unguarded smile as the memory of the night surfaced. Then his eyes flicked toward the corner where Lykaon slept. The smile vanished, replaced by a sudden flush of awkwardness creeping up his neck. He shifted, subtly pulling away, the memory of their shared space crashing into the light of day.

Just then, Lykaon let out a loud snort and sat up, rubbing his face with a groan. "Gods, my back," he grumbled, completely oblivious. "Sleeping on crates is a young man's game. Or a poor man's. I'm not sure which is worse." He stretched, his joints popping, and looked at them. "Is there any of that wine left?"

The mundane complaint broke the tension. Hanno let out a breath of relief. He was just Lykaon, crass and unaware. His secret was safe.

They dressed in the cramped quarters, a clumsy dance of averted eyes and turned backs. Hanno fumbled with the tie on his tunic, his movements stiff and unnatural. Lykaon, with a loud scratch of his belly, pulled on his clothes with a practiced indifference. Kallista folded her blanket into a neat, precise square, a small point of order in the chaos. They made their way to the ship's small mess area and gathered at a rough-hewn table for a breakfast of hard bread and dried figs. The silence was thick, but different from the day before. It was less a battlefield and more an awkward truce. And mental exhaustion. Lykaon ate with a gruff efficiency, while Hanno picked at his bread, carefully avoiding everyone's eyes.

As the men settled into their separate sounds of eating and silence, Kallista touched Lyrra's arm.

"Walk with me," she said, her voice a low murmur. "The air is better at the bow."

They left the men to their meal and walked to the front of the ship. The cool morning spray was a refreshing shock against Lyrra's skin. The sea was a vast, endless expanse of grey-blue, the rising sun just beginning to stain the horizon with shades of pale rose and gold.

They stood in silence for a moment resting against the ship's railing, watching the ship cut through the waves.

"Last night," Kallista began, her voice quiet, blending with the wind, "you were afraid of being seen. Of being heard." She turned to Lyrra, her look deep and knowing. "A fire is going to cast light no matter what. You can't shield it. It's just not worth the effort. It'll find the cracks—light always shines through. You cannot deny it. It's either you extinguish your fire altogether, or it is lit and casts light. So you might as well let it burn bright. There is no in-between."

Lyrra stared at her, the words a profound, liberating truth.

Kallista gestured subtly toward the sailors working on the main deck. "In the same way you drew Hanno into you, and he moved deeper, faster," Kallista continued, her eyes holding the wisdom of a master of her craft, "you can show men a wanting of them in different ways, and they will move in toward you, they'll share more quickly, more deeply." She met Lyrra's eyes. "You show them interest, you listen to them intently, and you stay quiet—and men will fill that space," Kallista laughed lightly. "They have a desperate need to fill things."

The thought landed with a sickening clarity, as if a floor had just given way beneath her feet. *My father.* He had never asked her a question in his life; he had only made pronouncements, filling every silence with the weight of his own authority. Gisco had been the same. She had spent her life—before Hanno—as a vessel for men to fill.

Kallista's voice was a low hum, her eyes fixed on the horizon as she spoke. "A man builds their 'fortress' with stoicism and strength—but the cracks are always there. A jaw that clenches when he speaks of a rival. A hand that grips a cup too tightly when a debt is mentioned. A glance that lingers a second too long on a map of home. A woman who can find those cracks … she can open any door."

"And what if the man is not proud?" Lyrra asked, her voice quiet and inquisitive, testing the waters of this new knowledge. "What if he's simply … tired?"

Kallista turned, her expression serene. "Then," she said, her voice soft, "you offer him rest. You become his harbor. And in that quiet space, he will show you everything he keeps hidden."

Just then, a sudden shout erupted from the main deck below them. A thick rope, frayed and straining under the tension of the mainsail, had begun to unravel. A burly sailor was trying to secure it, his face a mask of panicked concentration, while the ship's mate yelled orders at him, his voice sharp.

"They are easy to read, the men who work the ships," Kallista said, her voice a low murmur, barely audible above the din.

She gestured lightly toward the burly sailor with the rope.

"See how his shoulders bunch? He's afraid of not being enough, of failing in front of his crew. But his eyes … they stay fierce, his jaw set. That's what he's displaying to the others. He wants to be seen as competent, as strong. Respected. It's a performance. He's performing to hide his fear."

Lyrra watched, fascinated. Kallista's observations were like pieces of a puzzle.

The conversation lulled, but the space Kallista had opened remained. Lyrra found her own voice, hesitant but determined. "There are … other kinds of trust," she began, her eyes resting unfocused on the sea. "Other doors. I have heard sailors speak of … different types of pleasures. Between a man and a woman."

Kallista didn't flinch. Her gaze remained soft, accepting. "The body is a map with many roads," she said simply with a slight smile adorning her face. "Some are well-traveled. Others lead to quieter, more hidden places. They are not shameful. They are just … less known."

A hot blush crept up Lyrra's neck, but she pushed on. "They speak of it as … a violation. As something dirty."

"Anything taken by force is a violation," Kallista countered, her voice firm but gentle. "Anything given in trust is a gift. The back is no different from the front. It is simply a different kind of door. It requires more trust from the one who receives. More care from the one who gives. It demands slowness. Preparation." She met Lyrra's eyes, her expression frank and unapologetic. "And a lot of good, clean olive oil. The trick: *push out to let it go in*."

Blunt, practical advice, delivered with the same philosophical calm as her other lessons. *It wasn't dirty*, she thought. *It was a matter of trust.*

And logistics.

Kallista left her then, a silent retreat that gave Lyrra space for her own thoughts. Lyrra leaned against the railing, her mind working furiously, processing it all. The map of her world, and the map of her own body, had just been redrawn.

CHAPTER 15

The Price of Privacy

The midday sun beat down, bouncing off the surface of the sea. Lyrra stood at the bow, feeling the heat on her face and the slow, steady rhythm of the ship beneath her feet. Ahead, the hazy shape of Zakynthos grew steadily larger, a smudge of green and tan on the horizon. The overnight journey from Korkyra had been one of tense moments … and nocturnal pleasures.

Lykaon stretched, his joints popping with a series of loud cracks.

"My back," he gruffed, more to himself than anyone. "I'd sell my own grandmother for a mattress that isn't made of splinters." He caught Kallista's eye, and for a moment, his usual cynical mask slipped, revealing a flash of shared weariness. He pushed himself to his feet with a decisive grunt.

"Phormion!" he called out, his voice cutting sharply across the ship deck. "A word."

The brawny captain, his expression perpetually suspicious, turned from the helm. Lykaon strode toward him, with Hanno falling into step just behind, a silent, intimidating shadow. Lyrra and Kallista watched from a distance.

"We're offloading cargo and crew here," Lykaon stated, not a question. "That should free up some space."

Phormion's eyes narrowed. "Space is cargo. Cargo is coin."

"And my friends," Lykaon gestured back to Hanno and Lyrra, "need a private cabin for the rest of the journey. As do we." He hooked a thumb toward himself and Kallista.

A greasy smirk spread across Phormion's face. "Two cabins? Privacy is a luxury, mercenary. Luxuries are expensive." He named a price that would have rented them a comfortable room in a respectable inn for a week—a room that didn't sway, leak, or smell of fish.

Hanno tensed, ready to argue, but Lykaon held up a hand, a weary sigh escaping his lips. "For that price, I'd expect a complimentary bowl of exotic fruit and a girl to peel my grapes," Lykaon muttered, his voice dry as dust. "But fine. They get their cabin." He conceded the price for Hanno and Lyrra's privacy with a theatrical wave of his hand. "But that leaves a second problem. A practical one."

Phormion looked skeptical. "And what's that?"

"Me," Lykaon said, his voice deadpan. "I snore. Not like a man. No— Like a rockslide. Like a bear giving birth to a sack of anvils." He jerked his head toward Kallista. "The lady deserves a night's sleep without thinking the ship is breaking apart around her, and frankly, your crew will thank you for the peace of not having me in a shared space."

The corner of Hanno's mouth twitched. Phormion stared at Lykaon, first with suspicion, then with a look of grudging understanding. The logic, however absurd, was sound. An unhappy crew was a slow crew. He grumbled, "I can put you in the forward hold. It's empty and far from the crew's quarters. She can keep the cargo bay."

"Fine," Lykaon said, already turning away as if the matter was settled. He paused, then looked back over his shoulder. "And throw in a rope hammock. I'm not sleeping on the deck like a dog."

Phormion grumbled again, but gave a curt, dismissive wave of his hand. The deal was struck. Hanno stepped forward, discreetly pressing the heavy weight of the coins into the captain's hand.

The negotiation had secured them a temporary reprieve, a fragile sanctuary. It was a start.

They docked in an anonymous slip far from the main berths. This city was a crossroads, a place where ships came and went like tides, and where a man could disappear into the crowd. The air was thick with the smells of tar, pine, salt, and the distant, acrid tang of cheap wine.

The afternoon sun beat down on the deck of Phormion's ship, the endless, rhythmic creak of the timbers. Lyrra found herself leaning against the railing, watching the sailors below. A pair of them, weathered men with sun-baked faces, were arguing over a game of dice. Their voices were rough and loud, their gestures animated. Nearby, another was meticulously coiling a thick rope, his movements precise and practiced. A simple, mundane interaction. A crewman was carefully sharpening his knife, his brow furrowed in concentration.

Lyrra, still a novice in this world of veiled intentions, followed Kallista's example from earlier and practiced taking in the scenes. Observing the subtleties she saw in the interactions. She saw the captain's patronizing smile toward the dockworker, the man's forced deference. She saw the guards' rigid posture, a performance of discipline that felt almost brittle. Kallista's lessons weren't about seduction, but about seeing the truth beneath the surface. It was a different kind of power, one Lyrra was only just beginning to understand.

She was not just learning how to read men; she was learning how to read the world. And in doing so, she was beginning to understand herself.

It was a scene of ordinary life, of work and routine—and it struck Lyrra with a bittersweet force. She looked to the shore and saw a woman haggling over a basket of figs with a merchant. Her face was tense, and then softened into relief when the merchant finally nodded. She saw a child chasing a stray dog, his laughter bright and unrestrained. These were moments of normalcy, of simple, unburdened existence. A life she had sacrificed. A life she would likely never have.

The girl who had left Rome, the girl who had been just a placeholder, was still there, somewhere beneath this strategist, this lover—this fugitive. But she was haunted by the woman who might have simply been a wife, a mother, content with a quiet life. It was the quiet, aching recognition of the price she had paid for her freedom.

Hanno found her there, leaning against the railing, her eyes fixed on the horizon, her mind lost in thought. He came up behind her, his footsteps silent on the deck. He didn't speak, didn't try to fill the silence with platitudes. He simply stood there, his body a solid presence at her back, shielding her from the wind. She could feel the heat of him, smell the faint, familiar scent of salt and wool that was uniquely his.

"Look at them," she said, her voice quiet, her eyes sweeping over the bustling shore. She paused, the words catching in her throat as a sudden, sharp grief welled up inside her. "I— It's just—"

His arms came around her from behind, his hands covering hers on the cold, weathered wood of the railing. His grip was firm, his palms rough against the backs of her hands. He rested his chin on her shoulder, his breath warm against her cheek. He squeezed her hands, interrupting her before she had to find the words. He knew. He looked out at the vast, indifferent sea, and said, his voice a low rumble vibrating through her back, "Their life is written in chalk. Ours, we are carving in stone. Yes, it's harder. But it will last longer."

His words settled over her, and she felt the tight knot of longing in her chest loosen. She leaned back into the solid wall of his chest, the tension of her unspoken grief finally easing. He understood. He saw the sacrifice, this chosen path, and he accepted it. In that moment, his presence was more profound than any shared intimacy. It was a silent acknowledgment of the weight they carried, and the strength they found in each other.

A few hours later, as the sun began to dip toward the horizon, Phormion's ship weighed anchor. They set off on the final leg of their journey, a two-day sail to the distant, volcanic shores of Thera.

CHAPTER 16
A Vessel of Oil

Hanno was on watch. The ship, *Phormion's Fortune*, cut through the dark Adriatic, its sails catching the night wind with a steady, rhythmic snap. The sounds of the crew were muted, distant—the occasional shout, the clatter of a dropped tool, the low murmur of conversation from the lower decks. The sea itself was a vast, black plain, its surface rising and falling in a slow, deep rhythm. Its black surface occasionally broken by the phosphorescent glow of unseen creatures.

Lyrra found him leaning against the mast, silhouetted against the faint starlight. He looked weary, the lines of his face etched deeper in the dim light, but his posture was relaxed, the tension of the past few days having finally eased. He was Hanno, the merchant, the lover, the man who had shown her a strength she never knew she possessed.

She came up behind him, her steps silent on the worn deck. He didn't startle. He simply turned, his eyes finding hers in the gloom. A slow smile spread across his face, a genuine warmth that reached his eyes.

"You're awake," he said, his voice soft, rough with sleep.

"I was wondering where you went," she replied, moving to stand beside him, leaning her shoulder against his. The rough wool of her borrowed tunic felt familiar now, a second skin.

He reached out, his calloused fingers finding the curve of her jaw, his thumb brushing away a stray strand of hair that had escaped her braid. "The stars are clear tonight," he murmured, looking up at the vast, star-dusted darkness above. "You can see the constellations as they were meant to be seen."

"They are beautiful," she said, her voice a quiet breath against the night air. She felt the vastness of the sea around them, the endless sky above, and for the first time, she didn't feel lost. She felt anchored.

He turned his hand, his fingers lacing with hers. His grip was firm, his palm rough against her skin. It was the steady, confident hold of a man who was no longer adrift.

"We're still here," he said, his voice low, a rough rumble that vibrated through her. "After all that ... we're still here."

She leaned her head against his shoulder, feeling the solid strength of him. "Together," she agreed, her voice barely a whisper.

He kissed her then, a soft meeting of mouths that was more promise than passion.

"When this is over," he whispered against her lips, his breath warm, "when we're truly free ... I'll buy you that vineyard in Hispania. You can complain about the wine all you want."

A small, broken laugh escaped her. "It's a promise," she whispered back, her fingers tightening around his. She felt the truth of it settle deep within her, a quiet, unbreakable vow.

The quiet promise hung in the cool night air between them, a tangible thing. Hanno's hand tightened on hers, and he led her from the deck, down the narrow companionway to the small, private cabin Lykaon had secured for them.

The space was tiny, smelling of old wood and the faint, lingering scent of whatever cargo it had last held. But it was theirs. A door that could be barred, a space that was not shared. A sanctuary.

He turned to her in the dim light of a single, sputtering lantern. The raw emotion from the deck was still in his eyes, a deep, unguarded vulnerability. He started to speak, but she placed a finger on his lips, silencing him.

She had her own promise to keep.

Her hands found the ties on his tunic, her movements slow and deliberate. He mirrored her, his own fingers fumbling with the ties on hers. When they were finally bare in the moonlight, she moved to him, pressing her body against his, her breasts a soft warmth against the hard muscle.

"Every part of you is mine to know and trust," she whispered, her breath hot against his ear. "And every part of me is yours to know and trust. There are no shameful places between us."

A shudder ran through him. He turned, his mouth finding hers in a hungry kiss that tasted of salt and longing. His hands came up to cup her face, his thumbs tracing the line of her jaw. She answered his kiss with her own, a desperate, affirming pressure, her hands tracing the hard, familiar terrain of his back.

He broke the kiss, his breath ragged, and his eyes dropped to her breasts. He squeezed one, a possessive grip that sent a jolt of white-hot pleasure straight to her core. She gasped, her head falling back, and he followed the line of her throat with his mouth, his tongue tracing a hot, wet path down to her nipple. He licked it, then drew the hard peak into his mouth, suckling with a fierce rhythm that threatened to buckle her knees.

She was lost in the sensation, her fingers tangling in his hair, when he moved, his hands finding her shoulders. He was already hard, his erection a thick, insistent presence against her thigh.

It was in this moment, with her body already humming with pleasure, that her focus steadied. A spark of fear, of Roman shame, tried to surface, but she crushed it, Kallista's words echoing in her mind. *You want this. Lean into it. Let your fire burn bright.*

Her voice was a low, confident hum. "Lie on your back," she said.

He stared at her, a moment of confusion, then a dawning, heated understanding in his eyes. He didn't question her. He simply moved to the narrow bunk, lying back, his hands falling to his sides, giving her everything.

This was her turn. Her exploration. Her lesson to apply.

She moved onto the bunk, kneeling between his legs, facing him. She reached for the small lekythos Kallista had left for her, a vessel of olive oil—a quiet, knowing gift. She poured a small pool into her palm, the oil cool and slick against her skin. *It demands slowness. Preparation,* Kallista's voice echoed in her mind. *And a lot of good, clean olive oil.*

Her hands, now slick with the oil, moved to her own body. She traced the dark, shadowed cleft between her cheeks, finding the small, tight pucker of her asshole. *A different kind of door,* she thought, remembering Kallista's words. *It requires more trust from the one who receives. More care from the one who gives.*

She pushed a single finger inside herself.

An alien pressure. She let out a soft hiss of breath, her whole body tensing. She looked up and met Hanno's eyes. They were wide, filled with a reverent awe. He was trusting her. Completely. That trust was a sudden fire that burned away the last of her fear.

She pushed her finger deeper, then added a second, stretching herself, preparing herself. She was breathing heavily now, a continuous, broken sound, her head falling back as she focused on the feeling.

She withdrew her fingers, leaving herself slick and open and wanting. She took his thick, hard cock in her hand and slicked him with the remaining oil, her movements slow and deliberate, a reverent anointing. He shuddered in response to her touch.

"Lyrra," he choked out, his voice a raw plea. "Are you sure...?"

"I am," she whispered back, her voice an unbreakable promise. "Trust me. Be slow."

She rose into a squat and spun on her feet, using her hands to stabilize herself on his thighs. His muscles clenched to counter her weight as she lifted one foot over his body, then the other, lowering herself onto his lap straddling his hips, her back now to him. His cock flexed against her ass crack. She looked over her shoulder with a sly grin.

A clear view of my ass, she thought, a spark of unapologetic power shooting through her. *A clear, shameless invitation.*

Using one hand to brace herself on his hard flexing stomach, she shifted her weight, lifting herself slightly. With the other, she took his slick cock and guided it to her oiled backdoor. Lowering herself, she felt the incredible, resisting clench of her muscles. *Push out to let it go in,* Kallista's blunt advice surfaced in her mind. She took a deep breath and bore down as she slowly, deliberately, pushed out as she lowered herself. And with a shared, ragged gasp, he was inside.

Deep.

Gods. The feeling. It was an annihilation. A fullness. She was not just with him; he was in her, a brutal, shocking intimacy that went beyond anything they had ever shared before.

She stayed still for a long moment, letting her body adjust, letting them both feel the raw, shocking intimacy of it. Then, she began to move.

Slowly at first. A deep, steady, rocking rhythm. She controlled the pace, her hips moving up and down, taking him deeper, teaching him her body's language. She was learning it in the moment too. She leaned back, her hands finding his waist, feeling the hard muscle clench and release beneath her palms. His groans were no longer sounds of hesitation, but of an overwhelming pleasure.

She sped up, her own pleasure building, a gathering fire deep in her belly. This was a different kind of power. Not the defiant fire of Carthage, not the cold cunning of a negotiator, but the profound power of a woman who knew her own desires and was not afraid to claim them.

Her free hand, which had been resting on his waist, moved lower, her fingers tracing the line of her own slick folds. She found the small, hard knot of flesh, circling it gently. *The heart of the temple,* Kallista's voice echoed in her mind. *A pearl that holds the entire sea.* The new sensation, combined with the deep, stretching fullness of him inside her, was almost too much, a direct line to the core of her own power.

She felt the first tremors of his release begin, the violent, pulsing clench of his inner muscles. She rode him harder, faster, driving them both toward the breaking point. He roared, a wild, unrestrained sound of shattering release as he poured himself into her.

His climax triggered her own. A wave of blinding pleasure crashed over her, her own body convulsing, her own cry a sharp, triumphant sound in the small, swaying cabin.

She collapsed forward, every muscle in her body gone slack, her forehead resting on the hard plane of his chest, their breathing harsh and ragged in the sudden, profound stillness.

She just held him, her own body trembling with the aftershocks, the scent of them, musky and intimate, filling the small space as the ship rocked gently on the dark sea.

CHAPTER 17
The Frayed Hem

Morning light, a pale, watery gold, filtered through the single porthole of their small cabin. The air was warm, thick with the intimate scent of their bodies and the lingering, clean fragrance of olive oil. Lyrra woke slowly, not to a sound, but to a feeling. A deep, settled peace that seemed to reside in the very marrow of her bones.

She was lying on her side, facing him. Hanno was already awake, propped up on one elbow, simply watching her. The look in his eyes was not the hungry desire of the night before, nor the easy affection of their mornings on Issa. This was something else. A profound, unguarded reverence. The look of a man who had been shown a truth he never knew existed.

He didn't speak. He just reached out, his calloused fingers so light it was barely a touch, and traced a path from her shoulder, down the curve of her arm, to her hand. In this moment, it carried no spark of arousal. It was a touch of quiet acknowledgment, a physical sealing of the unbreakable trust they had forged in the darkness.

She laced her fingers with his, a silent answer. The shame, the fear, the last vestiges of the frightened Roman girl—they were gone, replaced by a quiet wholeness. They were a single, unbreakable unit, ready for the war to come.

They joined Lykaon and Kallista in the main cabin. The air had shifted. The quiet intimacy of the morning was gone, replaced by a tense, professional focus. Lykaon had unrolled a detailed sea chart of Thera on the table, its surface a complex web of coastlines, shallows, and soundings. He had weighted the corners with a whetstone and a spare dagger. It was a war map.

The four of them gathered around it, a council of fugitives.

Lykaon's finger, scarred and blunt, stabbed at the drawing of a sprawling villa perched on the highest cliff of the island. "Telemon's fortress," he said, his voice a flat, pragmatic rasp. "Built for vanity, but defended like a military outpost. Sheer cliffs on three sides. One road up, guarded by a gatehouse." He looked up, his slate-grey eyes meeting each of theirs in turn. "I counted at least twenty guards on the walls when I was here last. And that's just the ones you can see."

Hanno's eyes were fixed on the drawing of the villa, but he wasn't seeing the walls or the gatehouse. He was seeing the man inside. "He's arrogant," Hanno said, his voice a low, grim counterpoint. "Obsessed with his image. He doesn't just want to be powerful; he needs everyone to *know* he's powerful. He needs an audience for his victories."

Kallista, who had been a silent observer, spoke, her voice quiet and certain cutting through the tension. "Hanno is right. The guards are a performance." All three of them turned to look at her. "I saw it when we were there last year," she continued, her focus turning inward, remembering. "He held court in the market. He doesn't want power; he wants the *story* of his power." She met Lyrra's eyes. "That is his vanity." Her finger, delicate but sure, reached out and tapped the center of the villa on the chart. "And that," she said, "is the crack in his fortress."

Lyrra looked from the map to the faces around her. Lykaon saw the physical threat. Hanno saw the man's history. Kallista saw the soul. And Lyrra, her mind sharp and clear, saw how all the pieces fit together.

She leaned over the map, her finger tracing a path not to a weak wall, but to the very heart of the villa. "Then we don't threaten him with a sword. We offer him a mirror. One that shows him the man he desperately wants to be: the magnanimous victor, the master of his own story."

A slow, grudging smile spread across Lykaon's face. "A mirror," he mused, a flicker of genuine admiration in his eyes. "The man does love to look at himself." He tapped the drawing of the main gate. "So how do we get this mirror into the audience chamber?"

"We don't sneak it in," Hanno said, his voice now steady, the last of his earlier frustration gone, replaced by a focused energy. "We have it announced." He looked at Lykaon. "You walk in the front gate. You tell the harbormaster you have a delivery for his master: the notorious Hanno, and the trinket he stole. You've come to collect your bounty."

Lykaon's smile widened. "A performance. I like it. It plays right into his vanity."

"It gets us inside," Lyrra confirmed. "Once we're in the audience chamber, you will be the frontman," she said to Lykaon. "Hanno will be the shield." She looked at Hanno, a silent acknowledgment of his protective strength. "And I," she said, her voice quiet but firm, "will be the sword."

She turned to Kallista, who had been watching, a quiet, knowing look on her face. "And you, Kallista, will be our eyes. You will see the things the rest of us are too loud to notice."

Lykaon snorted, a dry, humorless sound. "Or *too daft*," he said, hooking a thumb toward his own chest. "Let's be honest."

The rest of the day passed in a state of quiet, focused preparation. The air in the main cabin, which had been thick with tension and argument, was now filled with the sharp, metallic scrape of whetstones on steel. Hanno and Lykaon sat on opposite sides of the room, each tending to his blades. They didn't speak. They didn't need to. The rhythmic *shing-shing-shing* was a shared language, a meditation on the violence to come.

Kallista, in contrast, focused on a different kind of weapon. She laid out the simple but elegant deep blue linen tunic Lyrra had salvaged. Lyrra watched as Kallista worked, her movements precise and thoughtful. With a small, sharp knife, she carefully frayed the hem, just slightly, to suggest the hardship of their flight. She used a damp cloth and a pinch of dust to subtly dull the vibrancy of the color around the shoulders.

"You must look like a fallen queen," Kallista murmured, her eyes focused on her work. "Not a common runaway. Disgraced, but not broken. It will confuse him. A man like Telemon understands defiance, and he understands submission. He does not understand dignity in defeat. It will be your shield."

Lyrra watched, then a slow, strategic smile touched her lips. She took the small knife from Kallista's hand. "And every shield," she said, her voice a low hum, "should have a hidden blade."

She turned to the tunic, and with a single, deliberate slice, she extended the slit at the side of the hem, raising it several inches higher than was proper. It was not a vulgar cut, but it was a daring one. A cut that would, with a certain turn of the hip or a casual crossing of the legs, offer a fleeting, tantalizing glimpse of a long, bare thigh.

Kallista looked at the new alteration, then at Lyrra. A look of shared understanding passed between them. It was a subtle, almost invisible weapon, designed to distract, to disarm, to make a powerful man forget he was in a battle at all.

When Kallista brought the evening meal of hard bread and salted fish, neither Hanno nor Lykaon touched it. Their focus was absolute, an unspoken ritual of sharpening the mind by denying the body before a battle.

Lyrra, however, took a piece of bread. She met Kallista's quiet look across the table. She ate because her fight would be one of wits, and it required a clear head, not an empty stomach. She needed her strength. Kallista gave an almost imperceptible nod of approval.

Later, as night fell and a sliver of moon rose over the dark water, Lyrra stood alone at the ship's stern. She held her dagger, the cool, familiar weight a comfort in her palm. She moved through the forms Lykaon had been teaching her, the simple thrusts and parries becoming more fluid, more a part of her.

But it wasn't just practice. With every movement, the memories surfaced. The sickening, fleshy resistance as the blade sank into the Mamertine's thigh. The shocking burst of warmth as it slid through Decimus's palm. She felt no horror. No regret. Only a cold, clear certainty. The girl from the villa in Carthage, the one who had feared a dropped crate, was gone. In her place was a woman who had stabbed two men in three days. This was the truth of her now.

She was still standing there, staring at the dark wake of the ship, when Hanno found her. He didn't speak, just came to stand beside her, his presence a solid warmth in the cool night air.

"That girl back in the villa, back in Carthage," Lyrra said, her voice a low sound that didn't break the stillness. "The one who thought sneaking out in a servant's tunic was the height of rebellion ... she's gone." She let out a small, humorless laugh. "That was only a few months ago. But it feels like a lifetime."

Hanno took her hand and laced his fingers with hers. "She had to be gone," he said, his voice a fierce rumble. "But she was replaced by this fierce, fiery woman." He squeezed her hand. "The woman I love." He raised her hand to his mouth and pressed his lips to it.

His words, an unwavering affirmation, were a gut punch of emotion. Tears dotted her eyes, hot and sudden. She squeezed his hand back, her throat too tight to speak. She thought of the simple, uncomplicated peace they'd just had on Issa, a lifetime ago, just days ago. The memory of waking to him mending a net on the veranda.

"Just—" she whispered, the words a broken, aching memory of a peace that now felt impossibly distant, "always save me the best fig."

He pulled her into his arms then, his grip tight. "Always," he said with a near silent whisper into her ear, an unbreakable promise. They slept in their cabin that night, a quiet, chaste intimacy, their bodies curled together not in passion, but in a shared vulnerability.

CHAPTER 18
The Marble Facade

Phormion's ship docked in the main, heavily guarded port of Thera with a gentle bump that felt like a death knell. The air was different here, drier, carrying the faint, sulfurous scent of the volcano that loomed over the city.

The four of them walked down the gangplank, every step a commitment to the plan, every step a deliberate move into the heart of Telemon's power.

Lykaon strode forward, a man born to command attention. He had donned the dark, burnished breastplate he had worn in Issa. In the bright Thera sun, the sigil on its center seemed to come alive, the bronze snakes of the Gorgon's head writhing with every step he took. He was a statement, a walking piece of his own deadly legend.

Hanno, his hands bound loosely in front of him—a convincing piece of theater—walked a half-step behind, his expression stoic and defeated. Lyrra and Kallista flanked them, playing their parts. Kallista was the quiet, unassuming consort, her gaze lowered. Lyrra kept her expression carefully neutral, her posture straight but not defiant, just another face in a mercenary's entourage.

Lykaon strode directly to the harbormaster, a portly man in a fine linen tunic who was overseeing the unloading of a grain shipment.

Lykaon's voice was a loud, arrogant performance for the entire dock to hear. "I am Lykaon," he boomed, his voice echoing off the stone quay. "I have a delivery for your master, Telemon." He gestured dismissively at Hanno. "A piece of property he has been searching for. And the trinket he stole." He paused, letting the weight of his words settle, drawing the curious eyes of the nearby guards and dockworkers. "I've brought my people to witness the transaction and ensure the terms are met. Send word to the villa. Tell Telemon I have come to collect my bounty."

The harbormaster, his eyes wide, gave a quick, nervous bow and scurried off, sending a younger runner sprinting up the winding path toward the cliffs.

And then, they waited.

It was a crucible. They stood in plain sight on the hot, dusty stones of the quay, a public spectacle for the entire port. Dockworkers slowed their pace, staring, lingering. Guards, who had been lounging in the shade, now stood straighter, their hands resting on their sword hilts, their eyes fixed on Hanno.

Lyrra kept her eyes lowered, her expression carefully blank, but her senses were screaming. She could feel the weight of a hundred pairs of eyes, the heat of the sun on the back of her neck, the coarse texture of the wool tunic against her skin. Every nerve was strained, every sound was magnified. The scrape of a guard's sandal on the stone. The cry of a distant gull. Each second was a distinct beat, a lifetime in which their strategy could collapse.

This meeting was the heart of their plan: a high-wire act of pure nerve, betting everything on the certainty of one man's ego, on his desperate need to savor the humiliation of his rival. If he refused them, if he simply sent his guards to take Hanno by force, they were finished.

A messenger, a young man breathless from his run, finally returned. He gave Lykaon a wide-eyed, fearful look, then bowed low. "The master Telemon will see you. Now."

The gamble had paid off.

They were escorted from the docks by a contingent of Telemon's personal guard. The procession moved up the steep, winding path toward the villa, a public spectacle that solidified their cover story. Lyrra kept her head down, her expression neutral, but her mind was a whirlwind of observation.

The villa was a fortress of wealth, perched on the highest cliff, a statement of dominance over the wild sea below. As they passed through the great bronze doors, the chaotic heat of the port was replaced by the cool shade and echoing silence of polished marble.

For a heartbeat the old fear returned—the familiar, sterile silence of a prison. A knot of ice formed in her gut. But then she saw the guards lining the hall, and the fear was instantly dismissed by a tactical clarity.

She looked at them, *truly* looked at them. Their armor, intricately embossed bronze, was polished to a blinding sheen, but it lacked the dents and scratches of real combat. The leather straps of their greaves were pristine, not worn with the sweat and grime of a campaign. They stood at attention, but their eyes were bored, their stances ornamental. *Local hires*, she thought, the clarity settling in her. *Dressed for show, not for a fight.*

They were led through a grand atrium. Unlike the rest of the villa's stark, militaristic opulence, this space was a testament to true wealth. Intricate Phoenician glass, glowing like jewels in shades of deep blue and sea green, was displayed in specially carved niches in the walls. The air smelled of a heavy, exotic incense she couldn't place.

The display was meant to awe, to intimidate with the sheer scale of Telemon's wealth, reach, and resources. And it worked. For a moment, Lyrra felt a flash of the old Roman awe, the feeling of being small in the face of such immense power. *No*, she thought. *Not power.*

Wealth.

He is peacocking, she realized, the thought sharp and absolute. *Just like Gisco, but louder. And more desperate. A truly powerful man has no need for such elaborate theater.*

The awe she might have once felt at such opulence was gone, replaced by a pragmatic understanding. This wasn't some stronghold. It was a stage. And the man at its center was no god. He was just a man terrified of being seen as small.

He was vulnerable.

As they turned a corner into a new, even grander hall, she stopped dead, a small gasp escaping her lips.

"Oh, dear gods," she breathed, the words a horrified whisper. She staggered back a half-step, her eyes wide.

Hanno shot her a sharp, questioning look. Kallista's hand subtly moved to her own side, a gesture of quiet readiness.

Lyrra just stared, her tension collapsing into a dizzying amusement. At the end of the hall, dominating the space from atop a heavy plinth of polished black marble, was a life-sized marble statue of Hercules, standing triumphant, one foot on the neck of the slain Nemean Lion. The work was technically masterful, but the god's chiseled, heroic face, with its sharp jaw and arrogant sneer, was an absurdly idealized rendering of Telemon's.

Lykaon looked where she was looking, and a low, performative whistle escaped his lips, drenched with sarcasm. He leaned into Lyrra, his voice a conspiratorial mutter just loud enough for her and Hanno to hear.

"Look at that," he breathed. "Telemon spent a fortune to prove he has the same taste in art as a drunken sailor with a head injury." He shook his head in mock sadness. "At least we know his ego is as big as his debt to good sense."

A genuine smile slid across Lyrra's lips before she suppressed it. The comment, a pinprick of cynical truth in the vast, opulent hall, broke the suffocating tension for a welcome moment.

The guards led them on, past the statue, toward a pair of massive, cedar doors inlaid with ivory. The air grew cooler, the silence more profound.

Two guards pushed the heavy doors open, the sound a low groan that echoed in the vast space beyond. They were ushered inside.

The audience chamber was a cavern of wealth and shadow. The only light came from high, narrow windows that cast long, dramatic shafts of sunlight onto the polished obsidian floor. At the far end of the immense room, a series of steep marble steps rose to a raised dais.

And there he was. Telemon.

CHAPTER 19

The Silken Net

Telemon sat upon a high-backed chair that was less a piece of furniture and more a throne, carved from a single piece of dark, gleaming wood. He was a man in his prime, his body lean and hard under a tunic of the finest Tyrian purple. He didn't rise as they approached. He simply watched them cross the vast, echoing expanse of the obsidian floor, a slow, predatory smile spreading across his face.

He was entirely focused on Hanno.

His eyes swept over Lykaon with dismissal, and over Lyrra and Kallista as if they were invisible, just mere chattel in the mercenary's entourage. His eyes, cold and dark, locked onto Hanno, and the smile widened. It was a look of pure, triumphant ownership.

"Hanno of Carthage," Telemon said, his voice a cultured purr that did nothing to hide the venom beneath. "Or should I say, Hanno of nowhere? I hear you left your city in something of a hurry."

He savored the silence, letting his victory hang in the air. He gestured to Lykaon. "You have done well, mercenary. You may present my property."

Lykaon walked to a small, ornate table near the dais and emptied the contents of a leather pouch onto its polished surface. The Star of Emesa rolled to a stop, black, absorbing the light of the grand hall. With the prize now on display, Lykaon gave Hanno a rough shove forward. Hanno stumbled, catching himself at the foot of the dais, his bound hands a public declaration of his defeat. He remained stoic, his expression a mask of stone, his gaze fixed on a point just past Telemon's shoulder.

Telemon's eyes glittered with satisfaction. He leaned forward, his voice a low, mocking purr. "Seven years, Hanno. Seven years you have been a ghost. A whisper. Tell me, how does a ghost manage to run so far, for so long?"

Telemon's question hung in the air, a gloating hook. Hanno remained silent, his jaw tight.

Lyrra saw Lykaon shift his weight, his mouth opening, ready to step in and play his part as the frontman. She saw Hanno's shoulders tense, preparing to endure the interrogation. She saw the scene playing out exactly as the men had planned it.

And in that split second, a choice, sharp and absolute as the edge of a blade, presented itself. *Do I let them do this? Protect me?*

Or do I burn?

Kallista's words echoed in her mind, a profound truth: *It's either you extinguish your fire altogether, or it is lit and casts light. So you might as well let it burn bright.*

She took a breath.

Burn. Bright.

She stepped forward into the shaft of sunlight, her movement so sudden and unexpected that both Hanno and Lykaon froze.

Telemon turned his attention to her, his eyes narrowing. The predatory smile faltered, replaced by a look of dismissive amusement. "And what is this?" he purred, leaning back in his throne, a king indulging a court jester. "Does the little stray have something to say?" He gestured with a lazy flick of his wrist. "Come closer, little one. I love it when pretty girls whisper into my ear."

Lyrra didn't react to the insult. She simply held his gaze, her expression one of unwavering focus. She walked forward, stopping at the foot of the dais, and then she waited.

The silence stretched.

She wielded it like a weapon, a void that Telemon, with his immense ego, could not bear. He shifted in his throne, the amusement in his eyes beginning to curdle into irritation. He had expected fear, or defiance, or tears. Or words. Something. Anything. He did not expect this unnerving, patient stillness.

"Well?" he finally snapped, the purr gone from his voice.

Only then did Lyrra speak, her voice full of a calculated curiosity that completely disarmed him. "The Star of Emesa," she said, shifting to look at the stone Lykaon had placed on a nearby table. "The stories they tell of it are incredible. They say your ancestors won it through blood and fire generations ago." She looked back at him, her eyes wide with a feigned, reverent awe. "Tell me," she said, her voice an inviting murmur. "Is it true?"

The question, a perfect blend of admiration and deference, was a bait Telemon could not resist. So unexpected, it threw him completely off-balance. The irritation in his eyes was replaced by a look of pleased, preening vanity. He had expected a confrontation; instead, he had been given an audience.

"True?" he chuckled, settling back into his throne, the master of his story once more. "My dear girl, the truth is grander than any story you have heard."

He launched into his performance. As the voice of the enthralled orator began to fill the chamber, Lykaon took advantage of the shift in focus. A quick slice of a hidden blade, and Hanno's hands were free. In front of them, Lyrra became the perfect audience. She leaned forward, her expression one of rapt attention, her eyes wide. She nodded at the appropriate moments, a silent, encouraging vessel.

Lyrra listened. She became a vessel, a quiet, empty space for him to fill with the weight of his own self-importance. Hanno stood behind her, a silent, intimidating shield, his hand now resting on his sword hilt, a physical promise of the violence held in check just beneath the surface of this conversation. Across the room, Kallista remained a still, watchful presence, her eyes missing nothing.

"My great-grandfather, Lycomedes," Telemon began, his voice taking on the sonorous, practiced tone of an orator, "was not like these other merchants, grubbing for coin in filthy ports. He was a visionary. He looked east, to the old empires, and saw not just trade routes, but a legacy." He gestured grandly, as if painting a map in the air with his manicured fingers.

Lyrra watched the way his hand, the one not gesturing, gripped the arm of his throne, his knuckles white, when he mentioned the battle. *He fears the very 'blood and fire' he boasts of,* she realized. *He's likely never seen real violence.*

"He sailed into the hornet's nest of the Syrian coast when others cowered in their harbors," Telemon continued, his voice rising with dramatic flair. "He faced the pirate fleet of the so-called 'Sea Demon' off the coast of Arados, a man who demanded a tribute of blood from any ship that dared cross his waters. They say the 'Sea Demon' had a hundred ships. Lycomedes had three. A battle that is still sung of in the taverns of Tyre."

He paused, clearly expecting a reaction. Lyrra provided it, a sharp intake of breath, a hand brought to her chest in feigned shock.

"He broke them," Telemon declared, his chin high, basking in her reaction. "Not with numbers, but with sheer, audacious courage. He rammed the flagship himself, boarded it, and cut the 'Sea Demon' down on his own deck. The Star of Emesa was the pirate's personal treasure. My great-grandfather took it, not as loot, but as a symbol. Blood and fire, my dear. That is how empires are forged."

The story is too perfect, Lyrra thought, her mind a calculating machine behind the mask of her rapt attention. *Too clean. Like the mosaics on his floor.*

Telemon finished his tale, his chest puffed with pride, clearly expecting a reaction of reverent silence. He got one, but not for the reasons he thought.

Lyrra gave him a moment, letting the drama of his story settle. A perfect imitation of a woman overwhelmed by the grandeur of his story. Then, she shook her head, as if in disbelief, her voice an admiring murmur.

"Incredible," she breathed. "A victory of courage. But what of politics? How did one man navigate the ambitions of the Diadochi?"

The question, a perfect validation of his ancestor's (and therefore his own) intellectual prowess, was a bait Telemon could not resist.

"Now, they were, uh … Sulli … Su..." She paused, her brow furrowing slightly, feigning a struggle to recall the name.

"Seleucus, my dear? Is that who you are thinking of?" Telemon grinned, eager to show off.

"Oh, yes—Seleucus, and, um … Tomah … Putoma…" Lyrra said, now covering her mouth in dramatized shame.

"Ptolemy," he corrected her, his grin growing larger. "You were so close, girl. But yes, politics..." he said, as if sharing a great secret, "…a far deadlier battlefield than the sea."

She leaned forward, her expression one of pure, wide-eyed admiration.

"The Ptolemies in Egypt were merchants at heart, their admirals fat and slow. Easy to outmaneuver." He waved a dismissive hand. "But the Seleucids … they were true conquerors. A different breed entirely."

"It must have required a genius," Lyrra said dripping with admiration and historical flattery.

He preened, puffing out his chest, his voice booming with the false modesty of a man utterly convinced of his own legend.

"A genius?" he chuckled. "He was a humble man. But yes, it required a wisdom that few possessed," he declared, his voice booming with false modesty. "A wisdom so profound that Seleucus himself sought my great-grandfather's counsel in Antioch."

Lyrra kept her expression one of rapt, unwavering attention, but behind the mask, her mind seized on the words. She didn't know the precise details of Seleucus's campaigns. It didn't matter. She wasn't listening to the facts. She was watching the man. And she saw it. Too neat. Too grandiose.

A lie.

Her heart began to beat a little faster, a slow, steady drum of dawning leverage. This was it. The first crack in his facade.

She needed to be sure. She chanced a glance at Kallista, who stood like a statue near the far wall, a silent, almost invisible observer.

Across the room, Kallista's eyes were still fixed on Telemon, her expression serene, unchanging. But as Lyrra watched, Kallista met her gaze and gave a single, slow, almost imperceptible nod.

A silent confirmation. *He is lying.*

Lyrra felt a surge of cold, thrilling power. She had him. She didn't need to know the truth. She only needed to know that he was hiding it. And now, she would begin to pull at the thread.

Lyrra turned her attention back to Telemon, her expression still one of wide-eyed, innocent admiration. She leaned into the lie, her questioning becoming more specific, more pointed, a silken net tightening around him.

She let a moment of awed silence pass, then leaned forward, her voice a soft, melodic hum, a surgical strike disguised as a compliment.

"Remarkable," she breathed. "To have the king's ear discussing maritime matters in the West when all accounts say his eyes and efforts were focused on Chandragupta in India to the East."

The seemingly innocent observation landed with the force of a physical blow.

Telemon froze.

For a split second, pure panic flashed in his eyes. He was trapped. He didn't know what she knew, only that she was questioning the very foundation of his story. He had been so lost in his own performance, so sure of his audience.

He tried to recover, to build a bigger lie. "Ah, yes," he stammered, his voice losing its smooth, oratorical flow. "The Indian campaign ... of course. But a king's attention is... it is vast. He was also concerned with... with the grain shipments from Egypt. My great-grandfather was an expert on the Alexandrian trade routes."

Lyrra didn't even have to look at Kallista. She could feel the lie unraveling, the desperate, clumsy patchwork of a man in over his head. He was contradicting the very story he had told moments before about the Syrian coast. The fear in his eyes was now palpable and desperate.

He was no longer a king on a throne. He was a cornered animal. And Lyrra, the quiet, unassuming woman he had dismissed as a piece of baggage, was the hunter who had just closed the trap.

She could have pressed. She could have asked another, more pointed question and watched him completely unravel. But she remembered Kallista's lesson. This wasn't about destruction. It was about control.

She pivoted. Her tone, which had been one of innocent inquiry, now shifted, becoming a confidential murmur, the voice of a co-conspirator.

"Your family's story is a powerful one, Telemon," she said, her voice a silken thread of an offer. "It deserves to be shared broadly, right?" Lyrra paused. For a moment her face went emotionless and her eyes widened looking straight at Telemon. Then it softened and her smile beamed bright. "Or," she continued, "the story could be *protected*."

The relief that washed over Telemon's face was so profound it was almost pathetic. He stared at her, his mind racing, finally understanding the true nature of the game he was in. She wasn't threatening to expose him. Not really. She was offering him an escape.

"What— what do you want?" he stammered, the last of his bluster gone.

"First, our freedom," Lyrra said, her voice calm and steady. "You will call off your hunters. All of them." She paused, letting the demand sink in. "And second, you will give us a new ship, and a contract. An *exclusive* contract for the shipping lanes between here and the Levant. You gain two of the finest merchants in the Mediterranean," she said, gesturing subtly to Hanno and Lykaon, "sailing under your name. A partnership. Their success becomes *your* success. Their legend adds to *yours*."

Telemon stared at her, his mind racing, searching for a trap. A final look of defiance sparked in his eyes. "And what's to stop you all from taking my contract and still whispering my secrets in every port from here to Hispania?"

Lyrra's smile was both sharp and brilliant. "Because, yes, a whisper would ruin you," she said, her voice low and conspiratorial, "but it would also ruin us. The contract you give us is built on the foundation of your reputation. If *your* great legacy crumbles, *our* profits turn to dust." She leaned forward, her final words a silken chain. "You are buying more than our silence, Telemon. You are buying our *complicity*."

Hanno, who had been a silent, coiled spring of violence behind her, let out a near imperceptible breath of awe.

Telemon stared at her, a rapid succession of conflicting emotions crossing his face: humiliation, fury, but above all, a dawning, grudging respect. She had not just defeated him; she had offered him a win-win, a way to save his reputation *and* profit from the very man he had tried to crush. It was a masterful, elegant checkmate.

"Done," he finally choked out, the word a surrender.

The tension in the room didn't vanish; it transformed. Telemon, the defeated man, was gone in an instant, replaced by Telemon, the master of the stage. He rose from his throne, his posture once again imperious, his voice regaining its sonorous, commanding tone.

"A new partnership requires a celebration," he declared, his voice booming through the chamber as if this had been his plan all along. "The city must see my magnanimity." He walked down from the dais, his movements once again regal. "And the return of my family's legacy." He clapped his hands, the sound sharp and final. A guard captain hurried to his side.

"Send a runner to the harbormaster," Telemon commanded. "The bounty on Hanno of Carthage is rescinded, effective immediately. And summon my scribe. Bring the Alexandrian ink and the good papyrus. We have a contract to record." He picked up the Star of Emesa from the table, his fingers closing around it with a possessive finality.

He then turned to them, a host once more. "You will be my honored guests tonight," he said, the words both an invitation and an unbreakable command. "We will feast to celebrate this ... new venture."

They walked out of the audience chamber, the deal secured. Hanno moved to Lyrra's side, his hand finding the small of her back, a touch of unadulterated pride.

Lykaon, who had watched the entire exchange in stunned silence, shook his head as if to clear it. He fell into step beside them.

"Seven years," he muttered, just loud enough for them to hear. "For seven years, I thought about how to solve this problem of Telemon. Swords, ships, spies ... It never once occurred to me to just send in a beautifully terrifying woman to get the man to talk himself into his own grave." He let out a short, sharp laugh. "I feel profoundly stupid ... and a little aroused." Kallista slapped his shoulder with the back of her hand as Lyrra and Hanno looked on. "What... It's a confusing time for me."

CHAPTER 20

A Reflection of Victory

The feast was a masterful performance. Telemon, the magnanimous victor, presided over a table laden with roasted peacock, honeyed dates, and wine served in his priceless Phoenician glass. He toasted his new *partners*, his voice booming with a false cordiality that was as transparent as that fancy glass. Lyrra played her part, a quiet, dignified presence at his side, while Hanno and Lykaon endured the charade with the stoic silence of men who knew the true price of the meal. It was an eternity of traded smiles and veiled threats, a final gauntlet they had to endure before they could truly be free.

Finally, it was over. A personal guard, his face a mask of professional deference, led them through a series of quiet, torch-lit corridors to a pair of massive, ornate doors at the far end of the villa.

"The master's finest guest suite," the guard announced, his voice a low murmur. He bowed, then retreated, his footsteps echoing down the long, marble hall, leaving the four of them in the sudden, profound silence.

Lykaon and Kallista gave them a quiet, knowing look. "We'll see you at the docks in the morning," Lykaon said, a rare note of genuine respect in his voice. He and Kallista turned and headed back down the corridor, leaving Lyrra and Hanno alone.

Hanno took a deep breath, the first truly relaxed breath he seemed to have taken all day. He looked at Lyrra, a slow, awed smile spreading across his face. He pushed open the heavy doors.

Lyrra's own breath caught in her throat.

The air that greeted them was warm, thick with the scent of jasmine and sandalwood. A private, sunken bathing pool, its surface steaming gently in the cool air, dominated the center of the space, the water a sheet of liquid turquoise. The walls were a sun-drenched, impossible glade, painted with masterfully rendered frescoes of laughing nymphs and lustful, goat-legged satyrs. On a raised platform at the far end of the room, a magnificent bed sat like an altar, its dark wood frame intricately carved, its linens a sea of pristine white.

But it was the ceiling that made her stop. It was a single, massive panel of polished bronze, so perfectly reflective that it cast a soft, golden, distorted image of the entire room back at them, a second, dreamlike world hanging just above their heads.

Hanno stepped inside, and with a quiet, definitive thud, he barred the heavy door behind them. The sounds of the villa, of Telemon, of the entire world, vanished.

They were finally, truly alone.

The thud of the heavy bar sliding into place was the most satisfying sound she had ever heard. Freedom.

She turned to Hanno in the warm, jasmine-scented air. The awe was still on his face, the look of a man who had just witnessed a miracle. A wicked and utterly triumphant smile spread across her own lips.

From the open balcony doors, a cool night breeze drifted in, carrying the distant, muted strains of a lyre and the faint, rhythmic clapping from the feast's lingering celebration. A fading outline of the performance they had just escaped.

"Well," she said, her voice a playful purr she didn't know she possessed. "That was a long day."

She walked toward him, her hips swaying with a newfound, deliberate confidence. She didn't stop until her body was pressed against his. He met her, his hands finding her waist, pulling her flush against him.

She reached up, her fingers tracing the line of his jaw, the rough scrape of his stubble a thrilling, familiar texture. To the distant, gentle music, they began to sway. Not a real dance, just a slow, quiet rocking, two bodies relearning their own rhythm after a day of forced, rigid performance.

He leaned his forehead against hers, his eyes closing. She felt the last of the tension finally leave his shoulders. He lifted a hand, his calloused fingers gently brushing a stray strand of hair from her cheek, tucking it behind her ear. His tender look was a universe of raw, unguarded emotion. Pride. Relief. Devotion. They didn't speak. They didn't need to. They just held each other, swaying in the moonlight, alone together on the other side of it all.

The music from the feast finally faded, leaving only the soft whisper of the night breeze and the sound of their own breathing. Lyrra pulled back just enough to look him in the eye.

"I believe," she whispered, her own eyes glittering in the golden, reflected light from the ceiling, "that the victor is owed her spoils."

A guttural groan rumbled in his chest, a sound of willing surrender. "Lyrra," he choked out, his voice thick with a desire so profound it was almost painful. "Anything. Whatever you want."

"I know," she said, and kissed him.

It was not a gentle kiss. It was a hard, messy, claiming kiss. A kiss of triumph. Her hands were in his hair, fisting in the dark curls, pulling his face to hers. His own hands, so used to leading, so used to protecting, hovered near her waist, unsure of their new role in this game.

She broke the kiss, her breath ragged, her lips swollen. "The bath," she commanded, her voice a husky order that left no room for argument. "Now."

A slow, dazed grin spread across his face. He didn't question her. He simply moved, stripping off his tunic with a frantic, eager energy, his eyes never leaving hers. She watched him, a deliberate inventory of the hard muscle of his chest, the taut lines of his stomach, the powerful V of his hips. He was a beautiful, powerful man. And tonight, he was hers to command.

She shed her own tunic, the fine blue linen sliding from her shoulders and pooling at her feet like a discarded skin. She walked to the edge of the sunken pool, the cool marble a shocking contrast to her heated skin. She dipped a toe in, then slid into the water with a soft hiss. It was hot, almost shockingly so, the steam rising around her in a cloud that smelled of jasmine and victory. She leaned back against the smooth, cool marble, a queen surveying her domain, and waited.

He followed, a willing captive drawn by an invisible thread. The water sluiced over the hard planes of his body as he sank into the pool in front of her. The heat was a shock, a delicious, enveloping embrace. Lyrra leaned her head back against the smooth, cool marble, a sigh of decadent pleasure escaping her lips. Her legs, light and buoyant in the water, floated to the surface. She let them drift apart, a shameless invitation.

He came to her, moving through the water, his eyes dark with a desire that was a physical presence in the steamy air. His mouth found hers again, but this time, the kiss was different. The frantic, triumphant energy was gone, replaced by a deep and utterly consuming exploration. His lips were soft, patient, tasting of wine and a victory that was now settling into a profound, shared reality.

His hands began to explore her body under the water, a slick, gliding touch that made her shiver. The hot water made her skin impossibly sensitive. His calloused fingers, so familiar, felt new and thrilling in this liquid world. They traced the curve of her hip, the dip of her waist, the soft swell of her belly. She felt the muscles in her stomach clench in anticipation.

He found her breasts, his thumbs circling her nipples, the gentle friction amplified by the water. She watched his face, the intense concentration, the unadulterated pleasure he took in pleasing her. Her nipples hardened into tight, aching peaks, and a low hum started in her chest.

She let him explore, let him worship, for a long, luxurious moment. She was the victor, and this was her tribute. She reveled in the feel of his hands on her skin, in the weight of his gaze, in the luxury of it all. The fear, the chase, the constant, gnawing tension of the past week—it all melted away in the jasmine-scented steam, leaving only this. This perfect, unhurried, and utterly intoxicating present.

But this was her game. Her victory.

She placed her hands on his broad, wet shoulders and, with a gentle but firm pressure, pushed him back.

"My turn," she whispered, her voice a promise in the steamy air.

She moved, her body slick and agile in the water. She rose from her reclined position, the water sluicing from her shoulders, and pushed him back, a deliberate pressure against his chest. He went without resistance, a willing captive, until his back was against the cool marble of the pool wall, his body half-submerged on one of the wide, underwater steps. The hot water lapped at his waist, his erection a hard spear breaking the surface.

She knelt before him in the water, the heat a comforting embrace around her thighs. Her eyes never left his. She watched the unguarded desire warring with a helpless surrender in his eyes.

She reached out, her hand closing around him under the water. He was hot, impossibly hard, a living, pulsing thing in her grasp. She stroked him once, twice, a slow and intense motion. A sharp, choked sound tore from his throat, swallowed by the steam.

Then, she leaned forward and took him in her mouth.

The sensation was a dizzying blend of textures and temperatures. The hot, slick water, the rough scrape of his hair, the smooth, yielding skin of his shaft. She took her time, a form of worship. She used her tongue, her lips, the gentle suction of her mouth, learning the exact rhythm, the precise pressure that made him tremble. His hands, which had been resting on the edge of the pool, came up, fisting in her wet hair, not pulling, but holding on, anchoring himself in the storm of pleasure she was creating. His hips began to buck, a silent, desperate plea.

She felt the first, tell-tale clench of his muscles, the sign that he was close, so close.

And she pulled back.

A broken sound of protest escaped his lips. He stared at her, his eyes dark, dazed, and utterly lost.

A wicked smile spread across her face. "Not yet," she whispered.

She rose above the surface of the water, it streaming from her body, her skin gleaming in the golden, reflected light. She climbed the marble steps out of the pool, a queen leaving her bath. She walked to the magnificent bed, her wet footprints a dark, temporary trail against the pale, cool stone. She didn't look back. She knew he was watching.

She lay back on the pristine white linens, presenting herself as an offering. The cool, soft fabric was a shocking, delicious contrast to her hot, wet skin. She spread her legs, the action a silent command.

"Come here," she said, her voice low and sultry.

He moved as if in a dream. He climbed from the pool, his magnificent body slick and gleaming. He walked to the bed, his eyes dark with a desire so profound it was almost reverent. He looked down at her, at the woman who had faced down mercenaries, who had dismantled a magnate with a whisper, who was now offering him everything.

He knelt on the bed, settling between her legs. She reached down, her hand closing around his hard, wet cock, and guided him to her entrance. He pushed forward, a perfect slide that made her feel whole. A deep, shuddering sigh escaped her lips. *This.* This was the spoils of her war.

She wrapped her legs around his waist, pulling him deeper, and they began to move together, a powerful and deep rhythm. It was a celebration of everything they had survived. Every fear, every wound, every moment of desperation was being washed away, replaced by this profound connection.

Her eyes drifted upward, past his shoulder, to the polished bronze of the ceiling. She saw them. A distorted, golden reflection of two bodies, tangled and slick, moving as one. A king and a queen, in their own private, ridiculous, and utterly perfect kingdom.

The sight, so decadent, so impossible, so utterly *theirs*, sent a fresh wave of pleasure through her. A laugh—a full-throated, joyous laugh—bubbled up from her chest. It was the sound of freedom.

The sound seemed to break something in him. The slow, reverent pace shattered. A groan tore from his throat, and he drove into her with a new, frantic energy, a joyful abandon. She met him, her own hips rising to meet his, her own laughter mingling with her gasps of pleasure. This wasn't just sex; it was a victory lap. A celebration of life, of freedom, of the sheer, absurd joy of being alive and together in this impossible, golden room.

She felt the pleasure coiling in her belly, tighter and tighter, a familiar, welcome fire. But this time, it wasn't a desperate release. It was a triumphant claiming. She was not just a survivor; she was a conqueror. And this, this man, this feeling, this moment—this was her empire.

She wrapped her legs tighter around him, her nails digging into the hard muscle of his back, pulling him deeper, demanding more. He answered, his thrusts growing harder, faster, a frantic, pounding rhythm that was a celebration of their shared victory. The sounds of their bodies slapping together, their gasping breaths, her own laughing cries, echoed in the opulent room.

She looked up at the ceiling again, at the golden, distorted reflection of them, a beautiful, chaotic dance of limbs and sweat and joy. The sight, so real, so *theirs*, was the final push.

The pleasure crested, a massive, unstoppable wave. Her vision went white at the edges. Her back arched off the bed, her muscles clenching, pulling him deeper, milking him. His own release was a raw roar that was swallowed by her mouth as he crashed down to kiss her, a shuddering, messy, laughing fall.

It was not a quiet release. It was a supernova. A screaming, triumphant explosion that left them tangled and breathless, their bodies slick with sweat and scented water, their hearts hammering against each other in the stillness of the room.

He sank down over her, still sheathed inside, all loose-limbed and shaking with spent pleasure. He buried his face in the curve of her neck, his own laughter a rumbling, breathless sound against her skin. She just held him, her own body trembling with the aftershocks, the scent of them—sweaty and hot, intimate and victorious—filling the warm, jasmine-scented air. They had not just survived. They had won. And this, this perfect, shared stillness, was their spoils.

CHAPTER 21
The Truth in Stone

They lay tangled in the pristine white linens, their bodies slick with sweat and scented water, their breathing slowly returning to a normal rhythm. The air in the opulent suite was still, the only sound the soft, distant whisper of the night breeze from the balcony.

Lyrra traced a lazy circle on Hanno's chest, her head pillowed on his shoulder. The frantic, triumphant energy had subsided, leaving a profound peace.

"That story he told," she said, her voice a low, sleepy murmur. "About his great-grandfather. The battle, the pirates … it was all a lie, wasn't it?"

He was quiet for a long moment, his hand stroking her hair. "The part about Seleucus, yes," he finally said, his voice a rumble against her ear. "You proved that. But the rest of it … I always thought it was true."

He shifted, propping himself up on one elbow so he could look down at her. A troubled, distant look entered his eyes. He replayed the scene in the audience chamber, the way Lyrra had unraveled Telemon's grand story with a sharp question. The lie had been so complete, so audacious … and it was that thought that surfaced a memory, a small, nagging detail from seven years ago. "Watching you today … the way you saw the cracks in his story, the way he crumbled. It made me remember something. A doubt I've had since the day I won that damned rock."

"There was a mark on it," he muttered, his expression uncertain. "I only saw it for a second that day, in the chaos of the race. I thought it was just a scratch, a maker's mark ... nothing." He shook his head, frustrated with himself. "But it wasn't his family's crest."

Lyrra's focus sharpened. "What do you mean?"

"A man like Telemon," Hanno said, his voice gaining a grim certainty. "A man that obsessed with his legacy, with his name ... he would have had his family's seal carved on his most precious heirloom, right? It would have been the first thing you saw." He looked at her, his eyes narrowed, his mind wrestling with the details. "But it wasn't there. It was something else. A simple mark. It looked more like a craftsman's mark to me. Or the sign of a guild ... a stylized ship's prow over a balanced scale."

Lyrra went completely still. The mark Hanno described was shockingly familiar. She had seen it before, not too long ago on her father's desk back in Rome. Pressed into the dark wax of a contract. Scrawled on the top of ledger pages. She knew this mark.

"My father," she said, "he had a contract dispute, a year or two ago. With a merchant guild from Tyre. They were accused of smuggling and piracy." She looked up, her eyes locking with Hanno's, the certainty dawning on her face. "That's *their* seal. The ship's prow for their fleet, the scale for their trade."

Lyrra watched Hanno's face carefully while he stared back.

"So..." he said, his words slow, his mind working. "Then his great-grandfather wasn't some visionary who *won* it in a battle."

"Was he just a common thief?" Her voice was an awed whisper, finishing his thought. "And bought it off a smuggler, inventing a grand history to go with it?"

He looked at her in wonder. "That *has* to be it. The Star of Emesa isn't some generational symbol of his *power*," Hanno said, the words now a complicated confirmation of their shared discovery. "It's proof that he really has *none at all*. It's the receipt for his family's original sin."

CHAPTER 22
The Sealed Message

The morning sun was bright, almost painfully so, glinting off the whitewashed walls of the city. The air was crisp, scrubbed clean by the night breeze.

The docks of Thera were a stage, and Telemon was its master. He stood beside them at the gangplank of a sleek, new merchant vessel, a ship whose dark, polished wood and pristine sails spoke of speed and wealth. It was their ship now.

Telemon played his part to perfection. He clapped Hanno on the shoulder, a gesture of feigned camaraderie that was a masterpiece of public performance. "A new partnership," he announced, his voice booming for the benefit of the watching dockworkers and the lingering, confused rabble who now saw their former prey standing under the protection of their master. "A new era of prosperity for Thera and the East!"

It was a masterful piece of theater, a final declaration that this had not been a defeat, but rather a brilliant business move. It was their safe passage, a shield forged from the very pride Lyrra had used as a weapon.

Once the performance was over and the contract signed and sealed, the four of them stood together on the deck of their new ship. The moment was heavy with unspoken words, the alliance born of shared desperation and sealed in victory.

Lykaon, for once, seemed at a loss for his usual cynical wit. He cleared his throat, looking out at the horizon. "The first shipment of wine from Naxos is due next week," he said, his voice a gruff, practical rumble. "Kallista and I will see to it. We'll manage the route." He finally looked at Hanno, a flash of the old, fractured friendship in his eyes, now tempered with a new, hard-won respect. "Try not to lose this ship," he said, gesturing to the wooden deck beneath his feet. "It looks expensive."

Hanno clasped his arm, a gesture of a promise renewed. "And you try not to spend all the profits before we return."

Kallista stepped forward and took Lyrra's hands into her own. "The sea is a storm," she said, her voice quiet, a soft, proud smile on her lips. "But you are a captain now. You know your own ship." She gave Lyrra's hands a gentle squeeze, a silent affirmation of the power they had discovered together.

Lykaon clapped Hanno on the shoulder, then turned to Lyrra, a grudging smile spreading across his face. "Well, General," he said, the title now a mark of genuine respect. "It's been an education. If you ever get tired of the shipping business, I hear there's a fortune to be made teaching wives how to terrify their husbands into submission. You could start a school."

He winked, then his expression turned serious for a moment. "And for Hades' sake, Hanno," he said, his voice a murmur, "let her handle the negotiations from now on. It's better for everyone's health."

With a shared look—an acknowledgment of gratitude, respect, and a friendship—Lykaon and Kallista turned and walked down the gangplank, leaving Lyrra and Hanno alone on the deck of their new life.

The ship pulled away from the dock, the shouts and smells of Thera fading behind them. The sails caught the wind with a sharp, satisfying crack, pulling them out into the dark, open sea.

Lyrra stood at the railing, the sea spray cool on her face. She watched the lights of the city shrink until they were just embers, then sparks, and then they were gone. She was now a partner in a new enterprise, sailing on their own ship, toward a horizon of her own choosing.

We survived. No. More than that—we won.

Hanno came to stand beside her, his arm wrapping around her waist, pulling her back against his chest. He was a warm presence in the cool night air. For a long, quiet moment, they just stood there, watching the dark, rolling expanse of the sea.

"We're safe," he murmured, his voice a rumble against her ear. "From Telemon, at least."

The words hung in the air, a quiet acknowledgment of the victory, but also of the threat that still lingered.

"My father is still out there," she said, her voice a quiet breath against the wind. "And Sybil."

The hunt from Hanno's past was over. But the hunt from her own, she realized with a cold certainty, was far more personal. And it had only just begun.

"My father won't stop," Lyrra said, her voice quiet but firm. "He's not a man who accepts a loss. He'll still see me as a stolen asset, a mark against his name. He'll keep sending hunters."

Hanno was silent for a moment, his grip on her tightening. "Then we can't just run," he said, his voice a grim echo of the decision she had made in the cave on Korkyra. "We need allies. Power. A place with so much wealth and history that even a Roman patrician's reach is limited."

He looked out at the dark, eastern horizon. "Egypt," he said, the word a promise. "Alexandria. A city of knowledge, of wealth … of secrets. A place where we can build our new life, and forge new weapons."

Lyrra nodded. The decision was made. They wouldn't just run; they would build an empire of their own.

Later, in the captain's cabin, Lyrra took out a small piece of papyrus. She wrote a short message, then sealed it with a drop of wax, pressing it flat. She added a heavy pouch of coins, more than enough for a long journey. At the next port, she would find a trusted captain to carry it on to Carthage.

The message was simple:

> *Asha, I need you. Meet us in Alexandria.*
> *- Lyrra*

With the message sealed, Lyrra felt the need for open air. She left the cramped cabin and went back to the deck. She stood at the railing, the cool sea spray on her face, and found herself staring at her own hands in the moonlight. She looked at them, truly looked at them. These were the hands that had learned to wield a dagger, to pleasure herself and her lover, to read a man's soul in a micro-expression, and to broker a deal that had won them their freedom. They were no longer the soft, useless hands of a Roman noblewoman. They were the hands of a woman who had fought, and bled, and won.

Hanno came to stand beside her, taking her hand in his. His own was rough, calloused, the hand of a fighter and a sailor.

"We won, Lyrra," he said, his voice a low, awed sound. "We're in control now. The power is ours."

She looked at their joined hands, at the contrast of their skin in the pale moonlight.

"I know," she said, her voice a profound whisper. "Now we have to learn what to do with it."

ABOUT THE AUTHOR

Sylvie D. Harlowe writes spicy romances that explore the fiery intersection of society, psychology, and unapologetic desire. With a lifelong fascination for ancient and hidden worlds, a keen insight into the human heart, and a love for sprawling landscapes and placid bodies of water, she crafts tales of fierce heroines who defy convention and heroes who are both supportive and utterly devastating (in all the best ways). Sylvie's writing delves into themes of reclaiming agency, examining complex trauma, the universal power of passion, and the enduring quest for a "happily-ever-after", no matter the era or obstacle. When she's not unearthing ancient secrets or plotting her next adventure across varying times and locales, Sylvie might be found admiring ancient coins, spending time with her family, or simply enjoying the quiet beauty of nature.

CONNECT WITH SYLVIE
@sylvie.d.harlowe
on *TikTok*, *Instagram*,
and other platforms.

ALSO BY THIS AUTHOR

A SERPENT & SPICE ADVENTURE Series

In the ancient world, where empires clash and destinies are forged in fire, one Roman noblewoman's defiance ignites an adventure that will span the treacherous Mediterranean.

Follow Lyrra, a woman who chose to spark a rebellion against an arranged marriage and a life dictated by others. With her is Hanno, the rogue spice merchant whose dangerous past holds secrets that refuse to stay buried, and whose gaze promises forbidden heat. Their love is a dangerous spark, a sanctuary, and a weapon, constantly tested by a world that hunts them.

The *Serpent & Spice Adventure series* is a high-heat, fast-paced journey where the stakes get higher, the locales more exotic, and the passion more daring with every book. Expect witty heroines who own their power, cinnamon roll heroes with a steel spine, found family that fights as fiercely as they love, and a romance that is tested, deepened, and explored in every possible way.

Book 1: Serpent & Spice
Book 2: Gorgon & Gambit
Book 3: Love & Legacy – Summer 2026

HEXUAL HEALING:
That Summer I Got Hexed by an Ancient Sex Toy

Releases January 29, 2026!

Her renovation project just got a lot harder... or not.

Penelope Bishop's plan for her first kid-free summer is simple: renovate the derelict Victorian mansion she impulsively bought with her 401k, and maybe, just maybe, get her life back on track after a soul-crushing divorce.

But when she unearths an ancient... artifact... in the dusty basement, her straightforward renovation gets a one-of-a-kind magical upgrade.

And not the good kind.

Hexual Healing: That Summer I Got Hexed by an Ancient Sex Toy is a laugh-out-loud, sinfully spicy, and surprisingly sweet paranormal rom-com—a witty and heartwarming journey into one woman's chaotic renovation of a crumbling mansion and her equally dilapidated love life.

This novel is packed with tropes you'll love: a hilarious found family, a unique "why choose (with science!)" reverse harem dynamic, small-town charm, a fixer-upper getting a second chance, and a healthy dose of spicy, supernatural shenanigans.

MY SAN DIEGO STEP DAD SUMMER Series

Lexi's just turned eighteen. Freshly legal. And dangerously determined to claim the one man she absolutely shouldn't want—her mother's husband, Adam. Now her mother's left for a three-week business trip, and Lexi's done waiting. She's an adult. She knows exactly what she wants.

What starts as a calculated game of forbidden seduction explodes into something neither of them expected: real love in the most impossible circumstances. This complete multi-book series follows their intense, scorching journey from that first explosive encounter through the consequences, confrontations, and ultimate reckoning that will either destroy them both or forge something unbreakable.

Book 1: Breaking Adam
Book 2: Double Life
Book 3: In Plain Sight –Winter 2026
Book 4: Counting Down –Winter 2026
Book 5: Make Him Watch –Spring 2026
Book 6: On Out Terms –Spring 2026
Book 7: His New Skin –Spring 2026
Book 8: Crashing His World –Spring 2026
Book 9: Erasing Adam –Summer 2026
Book 10: Burning It Down –Summer 2026
Book 11: Everything After –Summer 2026